STePheN FAiR

A Novel
Tim Wynne-Jones

A DK INK BOOK
DK Publishing, Inc.

A Melanie Kroupa Book

DK Publishing, Inc.
95 Madison Avenue
New York, New York 10016

Visit us on the World Wide Web at http://www.dk.com

Wynne-Jones, Tim.
    Stephen Fair / by Tim Wynne-Jones.—1st ed.
        p. cm.
    "A Melanie Kroupa book."
    Summary: At the age of fifteen Stephen begins having nightmares like the ones that drove his older brother away from home, and eventually the dreams lead to a discovery that is shocking but that ultimately allows his family to come back together.
    ISBN 0-7894-2495-9
    [1. Family problems—Fiction. 2. Nightmares—Fiction.]
    I. Title.
PZ7.W993St   1998   97-40328
[Fic]—dc21   CIP
                                                                  AC
Book design by Chris Hammill Paul.
The text of this book is set in 12 point Baskerville.
Printed and bound in the United States.

First American Edition, 1998
Simultaneously published in Canada in 1998 by Groundwood Books Limited.
10 9 8 7 6 5 4 3 2 1

This book is affectionately
dedicated to my own gang
of Usual Suspects.
The boys in the band
▼
Franc van Oort,
Jack Hurd,
Cam Gray,
and Peter Bigras

Acknowledgments

I want to thank Sylvia van Oort, who started the whole thing off by telling me, several years ago, an extraordinary story. Another good neighbor, Olga Zuyderhoff, introduced me to applied kinesiology and the healing practices of Dr. Edward Bach, especially his flower remedies. Thanks for that.

There really is an organization called FLAP, and I would like to thank two members: Edmée Steiner, for sending me some invaluable information, and Steve Price, who took the time to read an earlier draft of this novel and make some comments. The text has changed since then, so any mistakes in data are entirely mine. Keep up the grand work, Flappers!

My editors, Melanie Kroupa in the US and Shelley Tanaka in Canada, have been as insightful as ever and marvelously patient on this project. I owe them a huge thank you.

I would like also to thank Sarah Ellis and Kit Pearson, each of whom read the manuscript early on and helped me see into what was wrong with it and—more important at the time—what was right with it. Maddy Wynne-Jones holds pride of place as the very first reader of this book. Thanks, Maddy. And thanks to Amanda Lewis for steadfastly reading each successive draft. She continues, after twenty-three years together, to read me like a book *and* to read my books like me.

CONTENTS ▾

PART TWO

Prologue

Dreamcatcher

The nightmare announced its presence in the monkey cage with a low, drawn-out moan. Stephen opened his eyes. He glanced upward. The bunk above him creaked.

Marcus moaned again. There were words trapped inside the eerie sound, like something in a chrysalis fighting to emerge.

Stephen listened up. That was his job.

An arm flailed against the wall. *Thump*. Marcus shouted. "Stop!"

Stephen lay perfectly still, outside of the dream—beneath it—not daring to breathe.

A quick intake of breath.

"Go back, go back!"

Stephen edged himself up on his elbow.

"Doug?" called Marcus.

Stephen glanced at the clock on his bedside table. Two A.M. Doug and Brenda would be asleep. Unless they were still downstairs talking. There had been a lot of midnight powwows lately.

"Stevie? Where's Stevie!"

This was the part that scared Stephen: being drawn into his brother's nightmare. Unconsciously, he grabbed hold of the headboard as though he might be dragged along by whatever dream-current was tugging Marcus into deep water.

"Marcus, let it go," he said at last, trying to keep his voice calm.

There was a long silence. Then Marcus cleared his throat as though the nightmare had been a real thing lodged in his windpipe. He sucked in air greedily, a runner at the end of a race.

Stephen took a thick, bound notebook from his bedside table. He wasn't afraid to make a little noise now, as long as it was homey, comforting noise. He plumped up his pillows and sat up. He switched on the little wall light beside his head, blinked the sleep out of his eyes.

"Steve? That you?"

"Who do you think?"

"Was I making a ruckus?"

"A bit." Stephen opened the notebook to a clean page. There was a pen clipped to the cover; he clicked it open. "The tree house again, huh?"

He heard Marcus take a deep breath and let it out. "Yeah." His voice was groggy. Lately, it was always the tree house. But that was better than before, when it was just formless, nameless terror.

"I'm ready," said Stephen. His pen was poised.

"I was climbing down. Way below me there were people sitting around campfires, singing, playing guitars. Kids. You getting this?"

Stephen looked at what he had written: Ladder, campfire, people, guitars, kids. He would fill in the rest later. "Uh-huh."

"The music got loud. Made me dizzy. I was afraid I was going to fall. Then I saw Doug coming up the tree behind me. I yelled at him. He was in my way and I wasn't going back up. No way. But he just kept on coming."

"And then you called out to me," said Stephen.

"No," said Marcus. "You called out to *me*." He paused. "You did, didn't you?"

"I said, 'Marcus, let it go.' "

"Yeah," said Marcus after a moment. It wasn't what he remembered. "You called and I answered you." His voice was all dried up. "You got that?"

"Uh-huh," said Stephen. It wasn't as if he hadn't heard it all before.

Marcus was supposed to keep a log of his bad dreams. Details were important. He had handed the duty over to Stephen. "You're the writer," he said. Marcus was fifteen; Stephen was only eleven, but he had said, "Well, okay. Since I'm awake anyway."

Brenda had given him a blank book she had in the office: bound and everything but without any printing inside. Stephen called it Dreamcatcher. He'd written his name on the front as if it were his own dreams he was catching.

"No baby crying this time?" said Stephen.

Marcus thought a moment. "I don't know. The music was so loud."

Suddenly a door slammed downstairs. Sometimes Doug and Brenda's powwows ended that way.

"Thanks, Steve," Marcus said moodily. He turned over, punched his pillow a few times.

"It's okay," said Stephen.

But something wasn't okay, and it wasn't just the slamming door. Stephen looked at Dreamcatcher, open on his lap. The pages riffled as if there were a breeze in the room. Then they began to glow strangely, as if someone had switched on a light inside the book.

"Markie?"

There was no reply. He was alone.

The writing on the page began to dance before Stephen's eyes. He blinked. Now the letters writhed, curled up like pine needles touched by a flame.

"How can I write this down, if the words won't stay still?" he said. Then the edges of the page blackened and . . .

Whoosh!

Dreamcatcher was on fire. He tried to let it go, tried to push it away from him, but his arms, his hands, his legs wouldn't work.

This is so not fair, he whimpered to himself. They aren't my dreams! The book was blazing hot now, and the flames were licking at his eyes. Soon they would consume him. With a huge effort, he slammed the book shut. The room was plunged back into darkness.

And into that darkness Stephen Fair woke up. This time for real.

His hands were completely swaddled in his blankets. Dreamcatcher lay on his bedside table. There wasn't a whiff of smoke in the air. He untangled his hands, examined them in the dark, expecting to see them charred and still glowing. He lay back, staring up into the deeper darkness just above his head where the bunk had once been.

But not for four years.

He took a deep breath and switched on his light. He

hoisted himself up, took Dreamcatcher from the table. He opened to the last page with writing on it, half expecting to see Marcus's dream of climbing written there in the unsteady hand of his eleven-year-old self. What he saw was his own dream of the night before. Sometimes people spoke in his dreams.

"Don't say that. I hate it. Anyway, you were there, too."

He quickly turned the page.

How blindingly white it was. Empty, waiting. He opened his pen but the click startled him. He couldn't bring himself to write quite yet, fearful, suddenly, that the friction of putting pen to paper might be enough to ignite the book again. For what if this was just another dream within a dream and there was fire waiting for him wherever he turned?

Then the door of his room creaked opened. It was Brenda. Quickly he shoved the book under the covers.

"You okay?" his mother asked.

Stephen cleared his throat. "Sure. Yeah."

"Can't sleep, hon?"

Stephen rubbed his face with his hand in case his eyebrows were singed, his cheeks sooty. "Just the gnus again," he said.

She had asked him one day if his recent sleeplessness was like having hamsters running around on a treadmill in his head. "More like gnus," he had said. Better to joke about it. Better not to mention bad dreams. Or Marcus.

"We're going to have to do something about this," she said. "I think I know just the thing."

Stephen lay his head down on the pillow and let Brenda kiss him on the cheek. Then he burrowed down into his bedclothes. But he couldn't go to sleep, not yet. He must record his own dreams, just as he had recorded his brother's. And he must make certain that Brenda never saw them.

He didn't like the sound of "something about this" or "just the thing." He remembered what Marcus had gone through: the sleep clinic, the therapists.

Stephen would keep these dreams to himself. He shoved Dreamcatcher under his pillow. What would Brenda do, he wondered, if she found out that he had inherited his brother's nightmare?

Part One ▼

Stephen Fair

2 drops of cherry plum
2 drops of aspen
2 drops of honeysuckle
2 drops of crab apple

This is Stephen Fair.

That's what Hesketh Martin said. One of his mother's witchy friends. Big and brusque, carrying a huge cloth bag heavy with who knows what. Toads, Stephen thought. Puppy dogs' tails. He watched the bag to see if it hopped or wagged.

First she stood in front of Stephen with her palms on his outstretched hands, pressing on them as if they were levers on a machine. She frowned. She counted, pressed, counted some more, waved her hand in front of his chest to disturb his energy field.

Crackle, crackle went his energy field. From the way Hesketh drew her hand back, he was pretty disturbed, all right.

That's why Brenda had called in a witch.

"She's *not* a witch, Stephen," Brenda had warned him. "What she does is a perfectly legitimate form of alternative health care called applied kinesiology, and it may be just what you need."

He was going to go on, but Brenda closed her office door on him. On it hung a little needlepoint sign that read GO AWAY.

Hesketh levered Stephen's arms some more to pump his energy back up, or whatever.

Stephen yawned.

Then Hesketh plucked little glass vials of remedy from a wooden box and held them, one after another, near his chest to see which was the right one. It reminded him of going shopping for clothes for his cousin's wedding. The salesman had held up ties just like this to see if they matched his shirt.

Hesketh frowned again, as if she had read his thoughts and didn't like being compared to a tie salesman.

"What is it?" said Brenda, pressing close. "Have you discovered something?"

"Energy blockage," muttered Hesketh. She manipulated Stephen's arms some more, flapping them.

"*Caw, caw,*" said Stephen.

Hesketh smiled indulgently.

Finally she sighed. "I'm not entirely satisfied, but we'll give this a whirl, shall we." She had a British accent, which made her seem even more witchy to Stephen.

She mixed him up his very own remedy: a few drops of cherry plum, aspen, honeysuckle, and crab apple.

"This is you now, Stephen Fair," she said. "But things can change." Then she asked his body how many drops he needed and when. She seemed confused about the answers she was getting, as if there was a lot of interference. She glanced meaningfully at Brenda, who backed off a bit.

That seemed to improve the connection. Five drops in

water, whenever he liked, his body answered. Stephen hadn't uttered a word. He looked down at his body. "Traitor," he said.

Hesketh was writing down the treatment on the back of a business card. "What was that?" she asked.

"Just Stephen being cute," said Brenda.

The remedy looked like water. Stephen smelled it, wrinkled up his nose.

"There's a couple of tablespoons of brandy in it," Hesketh told Brenda. She was packing up to go. She seemed slightly flustered.

She stared Stephen right in the eye. She looked like a teacher peering through a peephole into a classroom in which the children were not doing their lessons but were throwing paper airplanes and running around. Then her expression changed. It was as if she had spotted one student in the very back row of that noisy classroom who was sitting very quietly, his pen poised, waiting for the lesson to begin. Again she stared at Brenda.

"What now?" asked Brenda.

But Hesketh's attention was on Stephen. "I'd like to see you again," she said quietly, solemnly.

Stephen didn't like the sound of that.

At the door Hesketh stopped and gave him the eye-at-the-peephole look again. She fished a booklet out of her cloth bag and handed it to him.

"I don't usually do this," she said, "but perhaps you should read up on the treatment I have prescribed and let me know if you agree with my diagnosis?"

He shrugged. *Dr. Bach's Healing Remedies*. The booklet wasn't all that fat. He took it. Easier than arguing. The business card was tucked in the pages like a bookmark.

And then she was gone, off on her broomstick (cleverly disguised as a lime green Ford Escort).

The cherry plum was for those who fear their mind is being overstrained, that reason is giving way, that they might do dreaded things. The aspen was for vague, unknown fears that something terrible is about to happen. The honeysuckle was for those who live in the past. The crab apple was for those who feel as if they have something not quite clean about them.

Stephen sniffed the bottle again. And what was the brandy for?

"Terrified? Living in the past?" Dom shook his head. "Apart from the not quite clean bit, this isn't you, Steep. This Hesketh woman is definitely whackoid."

They were at their place in the woods, a little room defined by a stream, a rotting log, a large, moss-covered rock. It was not a place they had built. It was a room constructed out of a geometry of branches and light.

"This Dr. Bach guy," said Stephen. "He'd make himself sick—"

"Just what you want in a doctor."

Stephen laughed. "Well, the way he puts it is, 'suffer a negative state of mind.' And then he'd just go and find the right plant to heal himself."

Immediately Dom jumped up as if the drama teacher had assigned him an improv. Holding his gut, he groaned and stumbled around. "Am I ever in a negative state of mind," he grumbled. Then he bumped into a tiny pine tree.

Sniff. Sniff, sniff.

Dom's face lit up. He tore the tree out of the ground, roots and all, and chomped off the topmost tuft.

"I'm cured," he shouted. "I'm cured."

Stephen thumbed through the remedy guide. "Pine is for those who suffer feelings of guilt," he read.

"Blcchk!" said Dom, spitting out pine needles and making a face. "I hope your stuff tastes better than this."

"Try some," said Stephen. They knelt by the stream. There was a pool about the size and depth of a washbasin there. Someone had attached a white metal cup to a string; it hung on a nearby branch. The cup's lip was rusty. Someone replaced the string now and then, but no one ever replaced the cup.

Stephen scooped up some icy-cold water and squeezed five drops of his remedy into it. "Go on," he said. "It can't hurt a flea."

Dom looked dubious. He sniffed.

"Brandy," said Stephen. "She never explained what that's for."

Dom took the smallest sip.

"Not bad," he said, smacking his lips. Then he crumpled to the deadleaf ground, curled his knees up to his chest, and rested his head on his hands. He had a big smile on his face, as if he were floating away to La-La Land. He snored.

If only it were that easy, thought Stephen.

He saw himself sitting up in bed while everyone in the world was asleep. But his bed was in the middle of the woods and the trees were filled with wind. Not wind but people, people in the trees, and the wind sound was their voices. He was in the trees, too, and his bed was rocking. And all around him, above the voices there was a sound as pure as springwater and just as skull-piercingly cold. A baby crying.

"Steep? Earth to Steep."

Stephen shook off the image, looked down at the ground, plucked at the yellow winter grass. "If Hesketh had taken me out to *look* for a cure, maybe it would have been a little more believable."

"Where does Brenda find these people?" said Dom.

Stephen chewed absentmindedly on a shoot of dry grass, then chucked it away. "Hesketh kind of schmoozed her way into Brenda's good books. She's the one who convinced her to go on that retreat over Easter."

"So is your mom sick or what?"

"No, the retreat's just a getaway. She's stressed out."

"It's been quite a while, huh," said Dom.

"What do you mean?"

"Well, remember your birthday party last fall? It was cool, but the whole time your mom looked like she was expecting the bad fairy to arrive any minute and lay a curse on you."

Stephen remembered, all right. His October birthday had always been a big deal for Brenda. It was as if every year she tried to outdo herself, to make it unique. His fifteenth had been no exception. Eight guys, two teams, paint-bomb war games in the woods. It was little-kid stuff, but they'd had a blast. Then there was a bonfire and, back at the house, chocolate fondue. But now, when he thought about it, Brenda had acted strangely. When had it started?

They didn't speak for a moment. The wind picked up, an early-March wind with a very clear memory of what it was to be winter.

Dom shuddered but his face lighted up. "But, boy, can she throw a party, huh? The best was two years ago—or was it three?—anyway, the time there was just me over and she woke us up in the middle of the night and took us to that all-night bowling place."

Stephen's face relaxed, glad to remember a happier time. Brenda had made them change in the dark into special outfits that turned out to be bowling team uniforms she had scored at the Sally Anne. They were shiny gold with black trim. They were hideous. And they were personalized. Stephen had the name Buck stitched on his breast pocket. Dom was Harold and Brenda was Dunc.

"What about Toni?" Stephen had asked, as they were leaving. There was nothing to worry about. Without the boys' even knowing, Brenda had snuck in a baby-sitter for Stephen's little sister. "As if I'd leave a baby alone," she had said.

It had been a magical night. The alley was miles away. It was after two when they arrived, but the place was packed. They had eaten hot dogs for breakfast at about five in the morning. By then Dunc had skunked them and attracted a fair bit of attention from more than one hotshot bowler. Stephen had never even known his mother could bowl.

"There's lots you don't know about me," she had said.

Tinkerpaw

Marcus had run away. He'd been fifteen, the same age Stephen was now, which made Stephen wonder if there was some kind of genetic malfunction in the Fair children. Time-release nightmares.

"It's natural at your age," Brenda used to say to Marcus. At first, anyway. "Lots of teenagers have nightmares. Teenagers and soldiers on the front line."

But things only got worse for Marcus, and it wasn't just the nightmares. The anxiety level in the Ark was high and rising with Doug and Brenda fighting their own battles.

Doug had built the Ark out of a dilapidated schooner, barnboards, telephone poles, wrecking-yard doors, greenhouse glass, and even parts of an old car or two. It looked like something Noah might have built without God's help.

Marcus and Stephen had shared a room, the monkey cage, it was called, on account of the two smiling monkeys Doug had carved on the door. But by the time Marcus's nightmares started, their monkeying-around days were far behind them. As the nightmares robbed Marcus of his sleep, he had grown irritable and disturbed.

So, on the family doctor's advice, Doug and Brenda took Marcus to a sleep disorder clinic. The doctors glued electrodes to his scalp, fixed an oxymeter to his ear to see how well his blood was saturated with oxygen, placed an electrooculograph where it could measure his rapid eye movement, and an electromyograph on his chin to measure muscle tension. There were sensors in front of each nostril, bands across his chest and stomach, electrodes on his legs.

And then they told him to go to sleep.

He was so nervous he had to get up to pee six times, and the technicians had to unhook him and hook him back up each time. He did sleep, some. The technicians didn't.

The sleep doctors decided that drowsy-making alpha rhythms were intruding on Marcus's deep delta-rhythm sleep. Marcus showed Stephen a little stretch of the polysomnogram, a chart as long as three football fields, where little pens had graphed out the shape of his sleep in an assortment of wiggly lines. The alpha waves looked to Stephen like a bad buzz cut; the delta waves looked like the jagged bottom of the sea.

The sleep doctors prescribed an antidepressant to get rid of the bad buzz cut so that Marcus could sink down into the restorative depths of delta oblivion.

What they didn't count on was night terrors.

Whatever was down at the bottom of his mind sent him hurtling back up to the surface screaming. Brenda would come to the monkey cage and hold him, but he screamed and screamed. A howler monkey. And Stephen huddled in the corner of his lower bunk in horror. In the mornings Marcus remembered absolutely nothing. But Stephen did.

It didn't take much to convince Brenda that they should dump the drugs down the toilet, which put an end to the night terrors. But reopened the nightmares' cage.

So they tried a bunch of less invasive therapists. They tried acupuncture and aura balancing. Next there was the mold man and the lady up north in the commune who waved crystals at him. Then there was the table rocker. The table rocker held a seance for Marcus to see if she could get him in touch with his dead grandfather. Doug had split by then, and Brenda thought that maybe Marcus needed a father figure around.

"Couldn't we just try Big Brothers?" he pleaded.

Finally, in desperation, they went to see a trick cyclist.

"A what?" asked Stephen. He was only eleven; he didn't get it.

"Psychiatrist—trick cyclist. It's rhyming slang."

"Oh."

Stephen's most vivid memory of that time was of Brenda driving home through a snowstorm. The trick cyclist was in the city, an hour away. Stephen had come along to get new shoes, and baby Toni had come along because there was no one at home to look after her. Toni was teething at the time and gnawed on Stephen's finger most of the way.

Brenda fumed as they crawled through commuter traffic and a white squall. "Freudians!" she muttered between curses. "I thought a woman doctor would be different. But no. They're all alike. It's always *Mother's* fault."

"She didn't say it was your fault," snapped Marcus. "She just said something went wrong."

They journeyed on into the vortex of snow, Brenda

pressed up against the steering wheel in order to see through a windshield half obliterated by ice.

"Of course you're anxious," said Brenda, her voice more hurt than mad. "Your father leaves—phhht!—but somehow *I'm* the one who traumatized you!"

It was the book that bothered her. Marcus sometimes took things to show the trick cyclist—things that popped into his mind—and this time it was one of his old picture books, *Are You My Mother?* It was about a little bird who hatches while his mother is away from the nest. The bird falls out of his tree and goes around asking forest creatures if they're his mother. He even asks a steam shovel.

Brenda didn't like the implication. "Have I ever deserted you?" she said.

"It's not about you," said Marcus. "It's about falling out of trees."

Baby Toni whimpered in the backseat. Stephen had taken away his finger. He dug out her bagel from down the side of the car seat. It was slobbery, gummed to death.

"I don't know what possesses me to waste my time on these quacks," said Brenda.

Marcus cranked the heater up to max, not for the heat but the noise. Stephen slumped back, leaning his head against Toni's car seat, dangling a bright toy in her face to distract her from her miseries. He let the churning warmth of the car's noisy heater lull him into the shallows below his brother's anger and his mother's unhappiness.

Marcus kept going to the trick cyclist. Brenda wanted to stop, but Marcus insisted on continuing. He liked his sessions with her. The free-association games, the ink blots, the weird collages. He took her books and photographs cut from magazines. And he took her his dreams, what there was of them. At first they were little more than fragments—sharp splinters. That's when the trick cyclist suggested that he keep a log.

Stephen liked that. A log. Something to cling onto to stay afloat.

"Yeah, well, how about you keep it," said Marcus. He had enough trouble getting through the night without homework. And so Stephen became the keeper of the log. The dreamcatcher.

He drew a picture of a trick cyclist on the front page. A stick figure on a unicycle crossing a tightrope. With Marcus on its shoulders.

Night after night Stephen was woken by Marcus's fidgeting, his moans, his shouts. He listened and recorded as best he could. And what took shape over a period of weeks was a story too fabulous to be real, part nursery rhyme, part fractured fairy tale. A village in the sky, a village of tree houses, a village on fire. Sirens. There were people in caftans, people in leather. Motorcycles, rock music. A baby crying up high in the trees.

It seemed it was the baby Marcus was trying to escape, climbing down forever but never reaching the ground.

Too unreal to have ever happened.

But it had.

Poor Brenda, when she realized.

"He was just a tot," she cried. "How can he remember that!"

* * *

The whole story tumbled out. She and Doug had quit university in Montreal, she English, he architecture, to see the world or as much of it as they could in a Volkswagen Beetle. They were on the road for years. Out in the Maritimes, working their way down into the States. Marcus was born in a commune in Tennessee and still his folks kept on truckin'.

Doug was into alternative housing. Wherever people lived in caves or domes or zomes or yurts or tepees or driftwood camps or fixed-up buses or broken-down windmills, he had to see it, had to help out, get his hands dirty. That's how they learned about Tinkerpaw.

Tinkerpaw was a tree-house village in the hills above Santa Cruz, California. It was named after a legendary junkman-builder down Big Sur way, though he had nothing to do with the village itself.

Doug loved it there. Brenda didn't. Tinkerpaw was too dangerous; she had a toddler to look after and a tree house was hardly childproof. But summer was coming on and Santa Cruz was beautiful, so they stayed.

Until the summer solstice.

The villagers decided to throw a party. The word soon spread far and wide. Days before the event, hippies from all over were showing up and camping on the hillside meadow just below the tree-house village. There was music. It was a festival. It was rumored that The Dead might come down from San Francisco.

By the night of the party, hundreds of people were there. It was too big, out of control. Bikers came; there were fights. And then, finally, there was wildfire that spread across the dry meadow and threatened the village in the trees.

The longest day of the year was turning into the longest night. It was a midsummer night's nightmare.

Brenda was frantic. Marcus was hysterical. Babies were crying everywhere, human fire alarms.

It broke Doug's heart to leave; he had put so much into the place. But there was no alternative. They were out of there, had to drive cross-country to avoid the cops. The "pigs," as Doug called them. Even as they were packing up to go, they heard the sirens.

They left Tinkerpaw behind. They drove all the way to Vancouver, where they started to get their life together.

"That's where I was born," said Stephen. The trick cyclist had asked him to come to the session, along with Brenda, since he had been the one who had helped to "winkle out the story," as she put it, by keeping the log for Marcus. It was a big task for an eleven-year-old. The trick cyclist was impressed, and Stephen was pretty proud of himself.

Brenda, however, was traumatized. Having to remember the ordeal at Tinkerpaw after so many years made her hysterical. She felt so guilty.

"Guilty about what?" The trick cyclist wanted to know.

"About exposing a kid to such danger," said Brenda.

"The fire?"

"Not just the fire, Tinkerpaw. Everything. Everything . . ."

The trick cyclist waited as if maybe "everything" had more to it. They all waited: Stephen and Marcus, too. But Brenda had nothing more to say.

"So leaving was the right thing to do?" asked the trick cyclist.

"Yes," Brenda conceded, stony-faced. "The right thing."

* * *

"The nightmares'll stop now," said Stephen that night, his tone confident. That is what he had been led to believe.

There was no reply from his brother in the upper bunk.

Marcus's sleep improved, but only a little. Knowing what had happened didn't seem to be quite enough.

Brenda apologized profusely. She apologized for exposing Marcus to such danger. She apologized for not recognizing sooner that it was the source of his trauma. She hoped Marcus would forgive them—except there wasn't any them now, just her. She asked if they could all just forget about Tinkerpaw. Marcus said he'd try.

But he still woke up a lot. And so did Stephen. He found himself reaching for Dreamcatcher with his eyes still shut.

"Steve? That you?"

"What is it, Markie?"

"I dunno," said Marcus. "Something." Then his big fist would hammer his pillow, trying to knock some comfort into it.

Maybe it was the Something that drove him away. Or maybe it was Brenda.

"We were kids. Crazy kids. We made a lot of foolish mistakes, but we learned from them. And you didn't perish there, Marcus. Let it go."

But Marcus couldn't. And he didn't know why. "There's more to it," he kept saying. And Brenda would hit the roof. He wanted to keep seeing the trick cyclist, who seemed to agree with him that there was more to uncover.

"This is what they do," said Brenda irritably. "They put ideas into your mind and then say they found them there."

She canceled the trick cyclist.

"That's enough probing," she said. "I've got a family to raise. By myself. I haven't time for this."

And Marcus left. They never heard from him again. It was terrible at first. It was as if he had died. Worse, sometimes, because of not knowing.

And now here it was, four years later, and suddenly Something of Marcus had stolen back into the Ark. Like a ghost with some haunt still left in him.

Why now? thought Stephen. Why me?

Virginia Elizabeth Dulcima Skye

Stephen stood with his foot on the first rung of the ladder, a series of planks nailed to the trunk of a tree. It was twilight. He looked up. He saw, through the tangled darkness of the branches, a platform far above him. That's where the crying was coming from. So far away, and yet it filled his head, a thousand tiny fists beating against the inside of his skull.

He took a deep breath, reached for the next rung. He felt himself rising, felt the gravity in what he was doing.

He stopped. How long had he been climbing? Surely not so long, and yet already he was fighting for breath. There was no air up here. Then how could there be sound? So much sound. The wailing from above and from below, the bickering.

"Don't say that. I hate it. Anyway, you were there, too."

"And I was too much of a wimp to stop it. Say it. That's what you're thinking."

No. He didn't want to hear this. He had to get away. He looked up and the platform was still just as far away as when he had started. His head was swimming, his arms ached, his knuckles were turning white.

He pushed on. He had never gone this far.

"Of course I care! You think I don't care? It's just that there should have been . . ."

"Should have been what? An angel, perhaps?"

Now the baby's crying drowned out the voices. That was something, at least. Stephen reached up again, encountering nothing but bare tree trunk. Panic seized him. He clung to the ladder, trembling. The rungs twisted under his weight.

"Hold on, Stephen."

It was a girl's voice. Virginia.

"I'm sure you can do it," she said.

He looked up again, encouraged by her faith in him. But the next rung was way beyond his grasp.

He dared to glance down. Virginia was taking something from a bag on her shoulder. A videocam.

"Don't give up," she cried. Her voice seemed so far away, drowned out by the unreachable crying child.

"Sorry," he said, though it was hard to say to whom he was apologizing. Then he closed his eyes and let go.

He fell and fell and fell awake.

His eyes flew open upon the impact of landing. The dream fall had knocked the wind out of him. He struggled to regain his breath. Gradually the starlight lent substance to the room around him, though there was still the deeper darkness directly above his head, where the bunk bed had been. Where Marcus had slept.

When Marcus had left, Stephen waited patiently to ask his mother if he could have the upper berth. He hadn't minded being on the bottom when his brother was there, but he felt oddly claustrophobic when the bed above was empty. Then, when he finally did ask her, Brenda broke down and cried and dismantled the bunk with a kind of triumphant sadness, as if tearing it down was some kind of dark victory over hope.

Stephen had tried to tell her that all he wanted was to sleep in the top bunk. But to Brenda, that bed had become some kind of a symbol. They would just have to face facts, she told Stephen. Marcus wasn't coming home. She put the unused bunk in the crawl space off the mudroom. Stephen didn't bother to tell Brenda that once she removed the bunk, the darkness remained. He kept the darkness to himself.

He had had a few bad dreams of his own when Marcus first ran away. Leftovers. The bunk had briefly made a reappearance. Brenda had decided that taking it away so suddenly had been too traumatic. As if Stephen's condition was just a problem of interior decorating.

But sleeping in the top bunk didn't help. In fact, he hated it. It made him feel nauseous, as if he were stranded high up on a stalled ride at the fair.

And sometimes he woke up certain that someone had lit a fire under the bunk.

"There *are* people who light fires under your bed," he cried in Brenda's arms. She held him so tightly he could hardly breathe.

"Shhh, darling," she said. "That's all over with. Those aren't your dreams, Stephen."

The upper bunk had gone away for good and the nightmares had stopped.

Now they were back. Not Marcus's leftovers anymore, but Stephen's very own. It was him on the ladder now. Alone.

Stephen settled into the ticking darkness. There was a difference. He always dreamed of climbing up; Marcus always dreamed of climbing down. He noted that in Dreamcatcher. What was up there that scared Marcus away and drew Stephen forward? Why could he never get all the way up? And then there were the snatches of argument. Brenda and Doug. What was that all about?

"How many times did Jack back off before finally tackling the beanstalk?" he wrote in Dreamcatcher. Maybe Jack, like himself, had a feeling there was something monstrous up there in the clouds. Maybe it was a really *big* baby!

Still, he had never climbed so far as he had tonight. And Virginia had been there. He wondered if she had caught his fall on her videocam.

Virginia Elizabeth Dulcima Skye. He had cruised by her house a few times. It was a big white split-level over in Meadowview Acres. Virginia's place was one of the few houses in that subdivision that actually did have a view of a meadow. It was the very same meadow that backed onto the woods where Stephen and Dom hung out. At the north end of the woods was the miraculous home Doug Fair had built for his family.

The Ark didn't float; it was just shy of water, for there was a natural pond at the foot of the Fair garden. The pond connected to a series of rivulets and streams and beaver-dammed swampland that stretched throughout the low-lying woods and out, finally, to the meadow upon whose flank Virginia's pristine white house stood.

Stephen closed his eyes. On a flood of fancy, the Ark pulled up anchor, floated silently through the moonless woods and across the meadow to Virginia's house, where the rising tide put Stephen's window abreast of Virginia's room.

And her light was on.

She was up late, invited him in. She was working on her project. He helped her with the gluing.

If Virginia had asked Stephen to come over and watch her compost rot, he'd have been there in a shot. He really didn't know her very well, except in passing. She passed him in looks and height and grades and on her way to volleyball games. He passed her in the hall as often as he could. This year they had the same English class, which is where he had learned her full name.

It was what Ms. Kettle had called "a name to reckon with." Lying in bed with his head on his arms, Stephen reckoned with it. Surely there was every letter of the alphabet in her name. No, no X. But there wasn't much missing. There wasn't much missing in Virginia, either.

He turned on his lamp. He dug Dreamcatcher out from under his pillow. Quickly—for it was dispersing already—he jotted down the main points of his latest dream. The baby, the ladder, the angry dialogue—what he could recall of it. There was always something new. Sometimes the dream started out entirely different. Sometimes Marcus was in his dreams and he was dreaming about Marcus dreaming. Very weird. Tonight the only new thing was Virginia.

He doodled a picture of her seen from high above. It wasn't very good. Then he wrote her name right across the next two-page spread, as befit its miraculous breadth. Nineteen letters.

VIRGINIA ELIZABETH DULCIMA SKYE

You could write a novel using just the letters in Virginia's name. People did things like that. Ms. Kettle had told them about some French guy who had written a whole

novel without using the letter E. Another guy had trans-
lated that E-less novel from French into English without
using the letter E, either. Maybe, thought Stephen, they
were people who didn't sleep much and had nothing better
to do with their time than think E-less thoughts.

Stephen wrote out his own name. Ten letters. Half as
good as Virginia's. So what could Stephen Fair do with his
own name?

Step. Hen. Fair.

Good start. All three syllables were words.

"I have begun the first step of a journey into the unknown," he whispered to himself. He wished he hadn't.
Being up half the night was one thing. Talking out loud
was spooky.

Snare, sharp, serpent . . .

Maybe Hesketh was right about his mind being over-
strained.

Fate, faint, free . . .

Maybe she was right about vague unknown fears.

Eat, enter . . .

He stopped writing. There was someone in the hall.

Brenda poked her head through the door before he
could hide Dreamcatcher. "You okay?"

"Sure," he said.

Then she saw the book in his lap and her face clouded
over.

"I'm just counting up the number of words I can find in
my name."

The news didn't seem to relieve Brenda.

"It's okay," he said. "I didn't hear a satanic voice telling
me to do it."

Brenda walked over to the bed, a wry expression on
her face. He closed Dreamcatcher. Her smile faded; the

sight of the book unsettled her. "Isn't that the old journal you—"

"Yep," he said, "but now I use it for everything. You know: drawing, stories, games . . ."

She sat down. She looked over at the bottle of remedy on his bedside table. "The level hasn't changed in days," she said.

"Amazing, isn't it," said Stephen cheerily. "I drink it and magically it fills right back up again."

Brenda looked contrite. "You think Hesketh's an odd-ball, don't you?"

Stephen tucked his knees up and opened his book so that Brenda couldn't see what he was writing. He trained his eyes on the list growing before him on the page: *Tap, tear, trap* . . .

"Okay, so you think *I'm* an oddball," said Brenda.

Pet, parent . . .

Brenda stilled his writing arm with her hand.

"Please don't shut me out, Stephen."

"I had this great dream," he said. "Dom and I and Virginia from my English class were cowboys. We all talked like Forgetful Jones on *Sesame Street*."

Brenda fingered the frayed edge of his bedspread. "I'm sorry I can't just leave you alone. I know that's what you want."

Stephen closed Dreamcatcher, clipped his pen to the cover.

Brenda's hair was long and black, her face as white as winter. "We should do some family thing," she said. "I've been so busy lately."

"Cool," said Stephen.

"Maybe I should cancel my retreat. We could go some-where, just the three of us."

Stephen tried to look enthusiastic. "It's your call," he said.

Brenda looked resentful. "Okay, okay."

She got up and walked over to the window, where the curtains billowed in and out on the spring night's breath. On a pedestal stood a sculpture about the size of an inflated beach ball but made of four intersecting copper hoops. It was called a Genesa crystal, and it was supposed to draw in positive life energy from a two-mile radius. Brenda held her palms open above it as if she were warming herself over a low fire. She had bought it for Marcus at a natural spirit sanctuary.

It started to rain. Brenda closed the window. The rain rattled on the glass, the tin roof.

Rain, thought Stephen. There was rain in his name.

"You're having nightmares, aren't you," she said.

"No way," said Stephen. "I get my best ideas at night, that's all. Probably just a phase I'm going through."

Brenda looked down and saw a banana sticker on the Genesa crystal. She removed it with her fingernail and scratched away the gummy residue.

She turned toward him, seemed about to say something, then took a deep breath and worked up a smile. In the shaded light of the bedside table, her expression seemed grotesque.

"I don't want any more pokers and prodders," said Stephen.

"No more pokers and prodders," said Brenda, crossing her heart.

Stephen worked up a smile himself. "Right on."

She came and sat again on his bed. She smiled radiantly at him, and yet the brightness was tinged with sadness. She touched Dreamcatcher. His grip tightened on it, clamping it shut.

Brenda looked alarmed but overcame it. She pulled her hand away, collected herself. "Does this mean you'll need tomorrow off?" she asked.

Stephen shook his head. "I have a project due."

A small voice drifted down the hall. "Steep?"

"Hi, Toni," said Stephen. He would have to add *steep* to his list once Brenda left the room.

"Party time," said Brenda. Toni appeared at the door, her own mop of black hair looking like the nest of a night bird. She came directly over to the bed and climbed aboard, wriggling between them for maximum comfort. She was as warm as a little fire in the chilly room.

Finally, Brenda scooped her up. There was a low rumble of distant thunder. Toni hugged her mother's neck.

Brenda turned to Stephen. "Sleep tight," she said, her lips curling in an ironic grin.

"Maybe if I tried straight brandy," he said.

"In your dreams, kiddo."

Alone again, Stephen returned thankfully to his list making. He was looking for *sleep* in his name, but it wasn't there.

No L.

"No el, No-o-elll," he sang. But he stopped pretty quick. What would Brenda think if she caught him singing Christmas carols in March?

Me, Myself, and Why

English was last period of the day. Stephen just made it.

The project was entitled *Me, Myself, and Why*. It was to be an autobiography in which the form of the presentation expressed something about the writer. "Do we have to tell everything about ourselves?" Gardner had asked. "No, Gardner," Ms. Kettle had answered patiently. "That would take fifteen years. You must invent yourself out of the facts of your existence." Everyone had taken that to mean there was a lot of leeway.

Joanna Carmody was going first. She had calligraphed her project on three sheets of art paper in mauve ink with hand-tinted photographs. Her biography began with the line, "It was a difficult birth."

"It wasn't really," she admitted. "I just liked the way the double Fs look together in the italic hand." It must have been the kind of truth Ms. Kettle had been looking for. She glowed with excitement and drew the class's attention—not for the first time—to Picasso's famous pro-

nouncement on art that she had framed. It hung just below the clock: "Art is a lie through which we perceive the
Truth."

The class hovered around Joanna's three calligraphy-
filled posters asking questions like, "How do you make
the pen line skinny and fat?" and "Was your cat really
mauve?"

Scotty went next. His project was a series of baseball
cards featuring Scotty himself on the front of each card in
a variety of baseball poses: slugging a homer, sliding into
second, scooping up a bunt. On the back, Scotty's life unfolded in a long list of statistics. Ms. Kettle had specifically
instructed the class that the writing could not be done in
point form. A couple of people mentioned this. But almost
everybody else, including Ms. Kettle, had to agree that this
was a perfect example of breaking the rules to good effect.

And then it was Virginia's turn. It took a bit of time for
her to set up. Stephen offered to help.

"Nervous?" Virginia asked him. He was hooking the
VCR up to the TV, but he couldn't make the connection.
Virginia didn't seem nervous at all; she seemed to bristle
with excitement.

"I'm taking as long as possible," he said. "The longer
your project takes, the more chance there is I won't have to
go until tomorrow."

"I bet your project will be great," she said.

"Awww, gosh, Miss Virginia," said Stephen in his best
Forgetful Jones.

Virginia's *Me, Myself, and Why* was brilliant. The video
was of her as a movie director being interviewed on *Entertainment Tonight*. She had arranged for Tiffany Ambleside, a
classmate, to interview her. Tiffany had hopes of becom-

ing a television star. Dom had suggested she'd be perfect as Vanna White's replacement on *Wheel of Fortune.* Tiffany had taken it as a compliment.

Virginia had done some slick editing to make it look as if the segment was really a part of *Entertainment Tonight,* dubbing words right into the mouths of Mary Hart and John Tesh, the show's cohosts.

In the interview, Virginia referred to herself as V.E. Skye. She was being interviewed, supposedly, on the sound stage at Universal, a busy director taking time off from a heavy shooting schedule. She was dressed in black, with a stopwatch around her neck and a clipboard under her arm, her long, straight, brown hair in a bun held in place by black chopsticks.

"V.E., welcome to *ET,*" said Tiffany.

"Thanks, T.A.," said Virginia. The class went wild.

"We're all dying to see some clips from your new flick, *Water & Main*—great title—but first, I'm sure our viewers would be interested to know your *real* name. Virginia Elizabeth Dulcima Skye? Certainly a name to reckon with. [More laughs.] So why only initials on the credits? And why not V.E.D. Skye?"

V.E. chuckled a professionally weary-sounding chuckle.

"Well, Tiffany, a movie screen—even Spectravision—is only so wide!" (A giggle from Tiffany.) "No, but seriously, Dulcima, my third name, comes from the Latin for 'sweet.' My father's idea. Which is cool but, you know, there doesn't seem to be room in my work right now for sweetness."

With that perfect lead-in, Tiffany faced the cameras and, with all her perfectly constructed teeth gleaming, announced *ET*'s exclusive preview of *Water & Main.*

A big-city back alley. Mean, wet. A siren somewhere.

The thrum of a motorcycle engine. The single headlight of a blue Harley-Davidson. A pony-tailed, middle-aged, hip-flask-swinging biker. A middle-aged waitress taking her break at the back door of a greasy spoon, smoke and light giving her dirty blond hair the nimbus of an angel.

"How'd she find adults to act in it?" someone asked, only to be shushed from every side. Then there was a gasp from someone in the back of the class, and a flurry of whispers. The couple in the scene were Virginia's parents.

Back to Tiffany and V.E. Yes, she admitted—for Tiffany had asked the very question that was on the lips of their classmates—she had cast her own parents in the lead roles of *Water & Main*. Her father, after all, was the drama teacher at the Catholic high school across town. Her mother now ran a catering service but had once been an actress. In fact, her parents had met at theater school. Yes, you could say theater was in her blood.

Stephen watched in delighted amazement as the interview continued, intercut with two more scenes from *Water & Main*. He assumed that the three scenes were all that there was of the movie, but that in no way diminished his amazement. Occasionally he glanced over at Virginia, whose gaze never left the screen. Her neck was strained forward slightly, her lips unconsciously parted, mouthing the words she had scripted for Tiffany, giving the answers she had scripted for herself. Only her hands moved. They were poised above her desk, her fingers itching to turn a knob, adjust some control, make it clearer, better.

Watching her watching the screen, something like melancholy came over Stephen. Where did she find the energy? To conceive of a project so colossal and then carry it out. *And* play volleyball.

His own project was folded up in his pocket. A single

sheet of paper, two copies: one for him to read out loud to the class; one for the Kettle to mark. He thought of Dreamcatcher, the writing he showed to no one. It wasn't just dreams. There were poems and stories that didn't go anywhere because the only place they had to get him was through the night. It all seemed so lame by comparison.

His wandering attention was suddenly brought back to the screen by a loud noise. It was a door slamming.

He looked over at Virginia, but her gaze never left V.E., never gave anything away.

On the TV screen, Tiffany was obviously confused. The noise wasn't in the script. She seemed to be looking to Virginia for direction. Do we go on? Do we do another take?

Bang. There it was again, another door, farther off. "High drama," said V.E. "That's what it's like in the movies."

Tiffany was slow to pick up on the cue. "I see."

V.E. turned suddenly to the camera, pulled a loose strand of hair from her eyes and tucked it behind her ear. She spoke directly to her audience. "I could edit this out, folks. But that isn't the kind of filmmaker V.E. Skye intends to be. This is Me, Myself, and Why."

She stared at the camera, daring it to flinch. Then, abruptly, she turned back to Tiffany. "You were saying . . ."

But Tiffany had lost her place. The smile had frozen on her face. It was as if poor Vanna White suddenly didn't know which letters to turn for the audience to see. "Thanks so much for your time," she muttered. Then, facing the camera, a stony look on her face, she said, "Back to you, Mary."

The screen went to black.

There was a moment of buzzing silence before the class

erupted in applause. Stephen led the clapping but he couldn't help wondering about the slammed doors. He knew all about slammed doors.

He glanced at the clock. If they could just keep clapping for ten minutes . . .

He stood, pulled the sheets of paper from his pocket. He didn't dare look at Virginia now. He found Dom across the room. Dom gave him the thumbs-up.

He placed a copy of his piece on Ms. Kettle's desk. He turned to face the class. He wished he had brought some music to play in the background. He wished he had thought to wear some kind of a costume, maybe a mask. He glanced at the clock. No bell was going to save him. His gaze skimmed over Picasso's declaration. Picasso wasn't going to save him. If he had been any less tired he would have panicked. He took a deep breath and recited as best he could.

> STEPHEN FAIR
> Nite.
> Ripe, she eats
> the arisen serpent
> He, a spear in the heat at the heart.
> First this, then . . .
> I rest
> in the She Sea
> the neat nest
> in the Fair tree.
> I stir
> Then strain.
> In sea, then in air—

Free!
I stare, I see
Parents, tears,
This sharp-seen star.
I enter the earth.
Steep in pain.

I is:
spine, tripes, hair, tears,
pee, shit, spit, fears.

I eat. In this I reshape the Earth.

Everyone sat in polite silence.

"Perhaps you could read it again," said Ms. Kettle. Obediently, Stephen did. She asked for comments, questions. Now the bell saved Stephen.

"Very succinct," said Ms. Kettle, kindly looking over the poem. "The assonance is compelling." Stephen gathered up his books. "Imaginative spelling."

He thanked her. Didn't try to explain. Maybe tomorrow.

Dom had rehearsals for Spring Follies. Stephen headed home alone. Suddenly, he heard his name being called and turned to see Virginia waving at him, waiting for the cars to pass so that she could catch up. She seemed intent on something.

"I am so angry," she said.

"I can explain."

"Explain what?"

"I don't know," said Stephen. "You look like you're ready to punch somebody out."

"Ooo, it's the Kettle," she said, falling in beside him, her long legs pumping. He hoped she wouldn't keep up her present pace. "She's nice but sometimes she's so dim."

"She loved your project," said Stephen. "She almost twittered about it."

"I'm not fuming about her reaction to *my* project," said Virginia. "I'm fuming about her reaction to yours. She didn't get it."

Stephen wasn't sure he had heard right. "Get what?"

"Your poem. All the words are made up of letters in your name. I wasn't sure, at first. 'Nite' threw me off. But I took a look at the copy on her desk while she was 'being supportive' to you. I mean, it's perfect. *You made a poem out of your own name!* You got at the very essence of the project."

Stephen didn't speak. He did notice, however, that the rain of the night before seemed to have polished the sky, which looked particularly blue. He noticed a yellow car passing by and thought how cheery it looked. He regarded a couple of children splashing in a puddle, a policeman laughing at a joke a motorist in a parked car was telling him, an elderly bicyclist whistling. And he happened to notice that the trees along the street were budding nicely, and the new leaves—the new leaves were extraordinarily crisp in outline.

A Vision in Orange

Like everything else Virginia did, she walked with an athletic intensity that left Stephen gasping for breath. He was glad when they arrived at her place. Had it been any farther he would have had to ask her for a piggyback.

The blue Harley-Davidson from *Water & Main* was standing in the driveway.

"It looks kind of out of place in Meadowview Acres," said Stephen, once he'd got his breath back.

"My dad is out of place here," said Virginia, but there was nothing crabby about the way she said it. Stephen regarded the house: white vinyl siding, black shutters, brass door knocker. Virginia followed his gaze, read his mind.

"The bike is Dad. The house is Mom," she said.

Dad appeared, right on cue. He wasn't in leather now, and his long reddish brown hair was loose. He was wearing jeans, ratty sneakers, and a Hawaiian shirt.

"Still in your work clothes," said Virginia, submitting to a fatherly hug. She introduced him to Stephen.

"Nice to meet you," he said. His smile threatened to

crack his face in half. It was a movie-star kind of face scarred by adolescent acne.

"Nice bike," said Stephen.

"It's a hog," said Lehmann. "Twelve hundred cubic centimeters of pure pigheadedness."

"Just like my daddy," said Virginia.

"Got a surprise for you, Dulce," he said. "Come on." He turned on his heels and headed around back. "You, too, Stephen."

Virginia made a face. "Did you see that twinkle in his eye?"

"Yeah," said Stephen. "Like he's built a trap or something."

Virginia gave him an approving look. "You catch on fast," she said. "The last time he told me he had a surprise, he had bought a pair of wolf cubs."

"Wolves? You keep wolves?"

Virginia shook her head. "The Meadowview Acres Tenant Association made us get rid of them. They liked to howl at the moon."

"The tenant association?"

"Idiot."

Stephen couldn't believe his luck. Fourteen hours ago, Virginia had been nothing but a dream. Now she was calling him an idiot. Progress.

At the back of the Skyes' house there was an upper deck and a lower patio. On the patio stood a round white table with a striped umbrella and three wrought-iron chairs. By the time Virginia and Stephen arrived, Lehmann Skye was standing smartly at attention with a burnt-orange napkin draped over his forearm like a waiter in a restaurant. He bowed extravagantly and, with a sweeping gesture, presented the table for Virginia's inspection.

Virginia groaned.

Stephen, on the other hand, was mesmerized. The luxuriously petaled head of an orange begonia floated in a crystal bowl of water. A bone white plate sat on a pumpkin orange placemat. On the plate a sliced mango had been artfully arrayed in a circle. There was a small, pale blue bowl filled with orange Smarties, and a tall frosted wineglass of orange juice with a little umbrella. The umbrella was orange. Everything was orange.

"Please accept my apology for the singular place setting, Stephen, but this is something more than a snack. Right, Virginia?"

Virginia scowled. "It's a lesson."

Her father grinned. "Such a discerning child," he said to Stephen. Then he offered to get him "a little smackerel" of something, too.

"Like Winnie-the-Pooh," said Stephen.

"Ah, a connoisseur of the classics," said Lehmann enthusiastically. Stephen beamed.

"Sorry there wasn't time to bake a sweet potato pie," said Lehmann as he hopped, two steps at a time, up the stairs to the deck and through sliding doors into the house.

Virginia slumped at her place, shaking her head. She took the tiny umbrella from the drink and spun it on its head like a top. It spun right off the table. Stephen picked it up.

"I made the mistake of saying I hated the color orange at breakfast this morning," said Virginia. "Dad made this big fuss about how a filmmaker can't afford to hate any color. I said well, maybe I'll just make blue movies."

Stephen laughed. Virginia picked up a piece of the mango and shoved it into his mouth. "You can laugh at me, but not at Dad. It'll just encourage him." She took a slice of mango herself.

"You've got to admit, this sure is orange," said Stephen. He had never tasted mango, but he had a feeling he was going to learn to like it.

"I love mangos!" she said. "And Dad knows it. I just hated the color orange this morning. I think it was my towel. It was gross. Who knows? Who cares?"

Lehmann cares, thought Stephen.

"He's pretty cool, really," said Virginia. "But sometimes he goes overboard." Her voice fell to a murmur as the sliding door above opened and Lehmann appeared with a tray.

Stephen found himself comparing fathers. His had the habit of going overboard, too. And then, one day, he just didn't swim back to the ship.

The tray contained more mango, another couple of glasses, and a bowl of Smarties—the nonorange ones.

"I'm sure Ms. Dulcima has explained to you the reason for this orange regalement."

Stephen nodded. "She was just saying how actually orange was her favorite color."

Lehmann laughed, a rich, theatrical kind of laugh.

Virginia kicked Stephen in the shin. "I told you not to encourage him."

Her father sipped from his drink—more amber than orange in color—then helped himself to a slice of mango. He held it up to the sun, squinted at it. "Truly, it is beautiful, is it not? No real artist would want to strike such a color from her palette."

Virginia scowled. "I'm not a *real* artist," she said. "I'm a teenager. Didn't anyone tell you that teenagers hate everything?"

"It's true," said Stephen. "I hate the number four. I had to go through a bunch of combination locks at school before I got one without a four in it."

Lehmann laughed toothily.

"I'm not allowed to hate anything," pouted Virginia. "Everyone hates something."

"Ah, but you're not everyone," said Lehmann.

Virginia glared at her father.

"My friend Dom was born in Argentina," said Stephen. "In his family they have a toast before they eat." Stephen held up his glass. "Death to our enemies!"

Virginia's face brightened. She held up her drink. "Death to our enemies!" she said, sticking her tongue out at her father. Lehmann joined in, clinking his glass with the others.

He looked hard at Stephen. "What else do you hate?"

Stephen thought. Being poked and prodded by witches came to mind, but he didn't want to get into that. "Work," he said, finally.

"Any kind of work?"

Stephen nodded. "Active stuff. Like turning on the television or brushing my teeth. You know, *work*."

"He's a writer," said Virginia.

"Ah," said Lehmann. "That explains it."

Stephen wasn't sure what it explained, but he was too intoxicated with joy to care. No one thought of him as a writer. Not since Marcus.

"He also hates being grilled by nosy grown-ups," said Virginia.

Lehmann reached out and squeezed her arm affectionately. "I've been teaching high school almost as long as you two have been alive," he said. "I know all about teenagers.

Don't get me wrong. I'm not down on the expression of strong emotions. Hardly! It's the word *hate* that I have a problem with. It's a door of a word. A big heavy steel door. Hate! You hear what I mean? Like a door slamming shut."

Stephen helped carry the dishes up to the deck and into the kitchen.

"Are you sure that isn't too much for you?" Lehmann asked.

Stephen made a show of laboring under his burden.

The kitchen was impressive. This was where Mrs. Skye ran her catering business. Stephen looked around. There were all kinds of gadgets, including a fax machine.

"What's this?" he said. "A pizza maker?"

Virginia patted him on the back. "Very funny," she said.

Lehmann chuckled while he placed the dirty dishes in the dishwasher.

When Virginia learned that Stephen lived in the woods on the other side of the meadow, she decided to walk him home.

"I didn't even know there were any houses back there," she said.

It's not really a house, he was going to say, but he decided not to spoil the surprise.

She put on rubber boots. The meadow was pretty spongy in the low-lying areas. Stephen said he didn't care about his shoes getting muddy.

As they were leaving through the gate at the end of her garden, Virginia's father called them back. He was standing at the door of the room off the lower patio. It appeared to be his study; the walls were lined with books.

He murmured something to Virginia and handed her an envelope, which she folded and stuck in her pocket. Then they were off.

"Nice meeting you," Lehmann said, waving at Stephen.

"It was very educational," said Stephen.

Lehmann chuckled.

"You don't have to try so hard," said Virginia.

"What?"

"To impress my father."

They walked in silence, wetting their knees in the tall grass, until they came to an old tractor path. They headed north, over the crest of the hill and down toward the low area that drained into the swamp gilded gold in the west-ering sun.

"Boy, that sun sure is orange," said Stephen.

Virginia punched him in the shoulder, but it was affec-tionate, as punches go.

"Sorry," she said, rubbing the sore spot. "It's just that people fall for my dad all the time," she said. "It's such a pain."

The tractor path dwindled to nothing. Stephen man-aged to keep reasonably dry through the wet lower field by leaping from one tuft of thick vegetation to another. Each tuft was like a stepping-stone, a million tiny islands in the boggy field. He explained that the grasses grew thick in tufts like that because that was where a cow had pooped. Every cow pat was a little island of higher ground.

"I'm going to make that my motto," she said. "Every cow pat is an island of higher ground."

They crossed the stream on a log, and Stephen wanted to tell her about his and Dom's place by the tiny pool. He wanted to offer her a drink from the little blue-rimmed cup. Then he wondered if she would think it dumb that he still hung out in the woods, so they passed by the spot without so much as a glance.

The path climbed upward and the woods grew thicker, darker, until the sun was lost to them, an occasional glimmering through the trees. Their passage flushed a grouse from the nearby undergrowth. It flew up almost in their faces, its wings thumping the air, startling them. Then another and another flew up and away, veering down the steep hillside to their left, into the snarled darkness of a heavily wooded valley. Stephen and Virginia watched until the woods had soaked up the last sight and sound of the birds' passage.

"If this was a movie," said Virginia, "the music for that valley would be played on a cello."

Stephen looked down the hillside, choked with bramble, clogged with the dead leaves of winter. In the blue-black shelter of the pine trees below, there was still a filthy crust of snow.

"Mordor," he said.

" 'Where the Shadows lie,' " said Virginia. "Mom and Dad and I went on a camping trip to Newfoundland and we took turns every night reading *The Lord of the Rings*."

Stephen's eyes hadn't left the woods. "I used to hang out down there," he said.

"How'd you get to it?"

Stephen couldn't recall. "I guess there were paths. It was a long time ago."

He turned away, in a hurry now, wanting to get back out to the light.

"Hey, wait up," said Virginia.

They walked in silence for a few moments. Stephen was thinking about what Virginia had said: "Mom and Dad and I." He never called his own mother anything but Brenda, had never called his father anything but Doug. It was something she and Doug had decided. They wanted to be known to their children as people, not as role players. Their marriage was not to be an institution but an organic, flowing thing, a living thing. That's what they said. Stephen thought about how there had been five of them in the Fair family. Then four, then three. An organic thing.

Virginia tapped the side of his head. "You still in Mordor?" she said.

They turned onto the old railroad bed that marked the border of the Fair property. Narrow-gauge trains had once run throughout these eastern forests. Now the phone company maintained the right-of-way for underground cables.

"Do you like films?" said Virginia.

"Doesn't everybody?"

Virginia shook her head. "Everybody likes *movies*. I'm talking about films."

"Oh," said Stephen. "Are films the thing they show at two in the morning and they're usually black and white?"

"Sometimes."

"I've seen a lot of stuff at two in the morning. Mostly I like to turn the sound off and make up what they're saying myself."

Virginia pulled from her pocket the envelope her father had given her as they were leaving. She handed it to Stephen. It contained what seemed to be an invitation to a party that Saturday night. The cover read "Round Up." When Stephen unfolded the invitation, it was a sentence: "Round Up the Usual Suspects."

"What is this?" Stephen asked.

"Do you know that line?"

"No."

"It's from *Casablanca*. It's my dad's favorite film. It's kind of my favorite, too."

Stephen had heard of *Casablanca*. He stopped, a bit flustered. "Are you inviting me to a party? Or is your dad?"

"Well, Dad beat me to it. But I was thinking of asking you. I mean, it's my parents' party, but I'm asking a few kids. But it's black and white. The film, I mean. Some kids can't get into black and white, so don't come if you don't want to."

They had turned off the railroad bed, onto an old logging path, and through the trees, finally, they caught sight of Stephen's home.

"Wow!" said Virginia, stopping in her tracks. "What is that?"

"The Ark," said Stephen.

Virginia was shaking her head in wonderment. "I've lived in this town all of my life and I never knew this place existed." She sounded disappointed in herself.

"You can't see it from the road," said Stephen.

"It's incredible."

Stephen stared at the Ark with new eyes, silently pleased by its tilting, crazy splendor. Nothing could have been less like the Skyes' place.

"It's got a tree growing right through the middle of it," said Virginia. "With a flag on top."

"Brenda made the flag," said Stephen. "It's Noah and Mrs. Noah on the ark, letting a dove go."

"There are word balloons."

"Yeah. Noah's saying, 'Go find us some land,' and the dove says, 'You got it!' "

"I'm awestruck," said Virginia. "Arkstruck." She laughed.

"Doug built the place," said Stephen. "He was my father. Is, I mean. But he isn't around anymore. It took him about ten years to build, then he took off."

"Men," said Virginia.

Stephen shrugged. "You're right. That's why I'm so glad that I, myself, am a Zorgon from Alpha Centauri."

Virginia laughed again, then turned her attention back to the Ark. "Well, I'm still Arkstruck."

So was Stephen. By the invitation. There was a grainy photo from the film. He recognized the face of the actor, but he didn't know his name. He was wearing a trench-coat, and his sad, handsome eyes stared out from under the brim of a fedora. Obviously "Round Up" didn't refer to a cattle drive.

The logging road made a lazy curve around the Ark, and Virginia's eyes never left the house glimpsed between the trees, as if she were intent on memorizing its every aspect. Then, just as they reached the end of the road, they heard singing and her gaze was distracted by a small girl standing in the middle of a puddle in the middle of the Fairs' driveway. It was Toni. She was outfitted in bright orange overalls tucked into black boots. Strands of her silky raven hair were wrapped in rainbow-colored embroidery thread.

She had a stick in her hand and was too busy singing and drawing in the mud to notice them.

"My sister Toni," whispered Stephen.

Virginia's face was beaming. "I want her."

"Be my guest," said Stephen. But he was joking. If Brenda was the ship's captain and he was the night watch, Toni was the engine at the very heart of the Ark.

"Her hair," said Virginia.

"She gets it from Brenda."

Virginia glanced his way and Stephen held up a hank of

his own lank, dirty-blond mop. "I take after my father," he said.

Virginia smoothed his hair back into place. "I hope not," she said.

Stephen looked perplexed.

"I mean, I hope you're not planning on taking off."

A Good Day for Canal Building

Toni wasn't drawing; she was canal building. The dirt driveway was full of potholes filled with rain. Toni was gouging a passage from one small pond to another, larger one. The larger pool had already drained many smaller tributaries thanks to her efforts. The fate of her dolly depended upon the success of her venture, for Barbie's boat had run aground. Her cruise had stalled, though she smiled benignly, glad to be on an outing on such a beautiful early-spring afternoon.

Toni suddenly stopped singing and looked up. "Hi, Steep."

"Want a hand?"

"No, thanks," said Toni, staring unselfconsciously at Virginia. "But she can help."

Virginia didn't waste any time. Following Toni's instructions, she found herself a good sharp stick and set to work.

"I'll sit over here with these other stones," said Stephen, perching on the edge of the nearby rock garden, looking miffed.

"Just as long as you don't get in our way," said Virginia.

"He's only pretending his feelings are hurt," said Toni. Then she busily started explaining what Virginia should do and where it was Beach Party Barbie had been heading before she ran aground. Soon Virginia was telling Toni about her own Barbies and how they hardly got to go anywhere anymore.

Stephen looked on, happy enough to be a spectator. Until today he had only dared to spy on Virginia. Now here she was in his own driveway, building canals with his kid sister.

"You're sure you're not hurt?" Virginia asked.

"No way," said Stephen, wiping an imaginary tear from his eye. "I'm not much on canals."

Besides, he needed the rest. It had been a long walk, a long day, and before that, a very long night. He had written his project sometime between two o'clock and six o'clock that morning, and yet it seemed forever ago. He could hardly even remember his own *Me, Myself, and Why*. But watching Virginia, he remembered hers.

There was a scene in *Water & Main* where the waitress climbed onto the back of the Harley and leaned her head on the biker's back. He tromped his foot down hard on the starter pedal and a kind of tremor ran through the viewers in the classroom—Stephen could feel it. She's not holding on! She's going to fly right off! That's what everyone was thinking. The waitress looked so vulnerable. But then, under the noise of the motor kicking over, came the sweet sad strains of an Annie Lennox song, "Keep Young and Beautiful," and the roar died down and everything went into slow motion. The camera angle was from below as if Virginia was in a hole, or something. How did she do it, Stephen thought.

"Ah, but you're not everyone."

Lehmann's words echoed in Stephen's head. He couldn't remember his father saying anything like that to him.

He never thought about his own father, but now he found himself trying to, trying to remember what he looked like under his shaggy, blond mane. How would he have filmed his father? Doug was always around, but always busy. You could help him out. You could hold the end of a board while he sawed, hold the end of a tape while he measured. But there was always a distance between you and him. Distance was what Stephen remembered most about his father.

Toni invited Virginia to dinner. "We're having schnitzel worms, smushed bunnies, and lettuce brains."

"Yum," said Virginia. "How exactly do you smush bunnies?"

"With a smusher."

"Ahhh, of course. I'll have to ask my mom if she has a bunny smusher in her kitchen. My mom's a cook."

"My mom's an editor," said Toni. "And they aren't really bunnies, they're potatoes."

"Ahhh."

"And a lettuce doesn't have any brains. It has dressing."

Just then the front door of the house opened. It was a wide door with carving on it, amidship and reached by a gangplank. Brenda appeared.

"Oh, hello," she said, her face breaking into a warm smile when she saw Virginia. And before Stephen could say anything, Toni introduced her new friend.

" 'Ginia," she called her. "This is Mom."

That was another thing about Toni: She had never bought into addressing her mother by her first name.

Doug was gone before she could say Dada, but Brenda never weaned her of the Mom thing. Toni had a mind of her own.

Virginia was explaining why, as much as she loved schnitzel worms, she couldn't stay for dinner. Stephen watched the three of them talk at the foot of the gangplank as though it were a show on TV. He felt a little left out. Distant.

Toni turned to look his way. They all did. He waved. Virginia waved back, but it seemed that Toni and Brenda were looking for something else. He looked around, following their gaze. At the far corner of the rock garden sat a pile of letters.

Stephen went to get them.

"This what you're looking for?"

Brenda nodded. Toni sagged with relief against her mother's side. She must have been on her way back from the mailbox when Barbie's distress sidetracked her.

Stephen sorted through the letters as he approached the Ark. Among the junk mail, bills, and work-related stuff addressed to "Ark Writing Services," there was a letter to Brenda from Nan. Her name wasn't on it, but Stephen recognized the return address in the city. It had been a long time since he had been to Olive Place.

Nan was Doug's mother. The last Stephen had heard from her was at Christmas. She always wrote at Christmas and on their birthdays. Stephen always sent her a homemade Christmas card which she never failed to admire. Otherwise, they hadn't seen each other in a couple of years. Nobody said as much, but he didn't think Brenda and Nan really got along too well. He could tell; if you made too much of a fuss over a gift she had sent, you could see what it did to Brenda, even if she tried to hide it. Just another one of those awkward things that didn't get talked about.

Nan never forgot important occasions. Doug, on the other hand, hardly ever remembered. His letters were rare, and they were from places like Guatemala and Kicking Horse Pass.

How wobbly Nan's handwriting was. Stephen wondered if she had grown infirm. Hard to imagine Nan slowed down; she had always been an active sort. So what important occasion was it that made her write to Brenda?

Toni met him halfway and took the letters to Brenda, who had her arms folded on her chest and was tapping her foot as if she were cross.

Virginia patted Toni on the shoulder. "Thanks for letting me help out," she said. "My folks are going to be wondering where I am."

Toni made her promise to come around again. Virginia glanced at Stephen.

"We'll keep your stick in the shed," he said.

"He means the dinghy," said Toni. "The shed is called the dinghy. You want to see it?"

Virginia said she'd love to another time.

Brenda, meanwhile, with a quick good-bye, headed back into the house. Something in the mail obviously required her immediate attention.

Stephen walked Virginia out to the road. She wasn't sure she would be able to find her way back through the woods, so she was going to take the long way around.

"Thanks," he said.

"For what?"

"For understanding 'Stephen Fair.' "

It took her a moment to catch his meaning. "My pleasure," she said. Then she set off. But she turned back to him. "Did you hate your dad when he left?"

Stephen was caught off guard.

"I guess that was pretty blunt," said Virginia. "Sorry."

"No, it's okay," said Stephen. "I was just thinking about him, so it sort of surprised me."

"How long has it been?"

"Just over four years. Did I hate him . . . No, I don't think so. It was . . . What? Like he had been going for a long time. Or maybe like he hadn't really been here? I don't know."

Virginia glanced toward the Ark and Stephen caught the gist of what she was thinking.

"Yeah, I know. He built us one amazing house. He was an amazing person, I guess. And he was around—a lot of fathers aren't. But he was around and not around, if you know what I mean."

Virginia nodded. "Sometimes I think my father is *too* around." Then her face clouded. "But if he left us, I don't know what I'd do."

Over dinner, the Fairs talked about Virginia. Toni did most of the talking, as if she and Virginia were old buds. They seemed to have covered a lot of ground together that afternoon.

"Mom, are you listening?"

Brenda was picking at her meal. "Hmm?"

Toni held her empty water glass to her eye. "I said 'Ginia's going to make a movie of me."

"Oh, that's lovely," said Brenda, but her mind was elsewhere.

"Gosh!" said Toni. She was observing her mother

through the bottom of her glass. "You have a whole bunch of faces!"

"And all of them want you to eat your dinner."

Toni put down her glass.

"Is there some bad news?" Stephen asked.

Brenda regarded him suspiciously. "What makes you say that?"

"I thought maybe . . . in the mail . . ."

Brenda seemed flustered for a moment. "Oh, not bad news. My application for the retreat has been accepted. But I'm just not sure about it anymore."

"What's a retreat?" asked Toni. She was making a mountain out of her smushed bunnies.

"A place for contemplation," said Brenda.

"What?"

"A getaway," said Stephen, "where there are no five-year-olds so a person can think."

"Can't you think, Mommy?"

Brenda smiled wearily. "Far too much. That's my problem."

"So have you changed your mind about going?" Stephen asked. While she was away, Stephen was going to the city with Dom's family and Toni was going to stay at her friend Dee's.

Brenda shrugged. "I've never left you guys," she said.

"It's just three days," said Stephen. He was really looking forward to going to the city. "It'll be great."

"Will it?" asked Brenda. But she wasn't speaking to Stephen.

Stephen helped her with the dishes that night. They worked in silence for a while, but Stephen couldn't shake the feeling that there was something she wanted to ask him or tell him.

"What's up, Brenda?"

She stopped drying, hung the tea towel on its hook. "I had coffee with Hesketh Martin today."

So that was it.

"She was wondering whether you had been able to read the booklet she left you."

Stephen pulled the plug and watched the dirty water drain out of the sink. "I read it," he said. "I think her diagnosis is a load of cow poop."

"That's interesting," said Brenda.

"Sorry," said Stephen.

"That's okay," said Brenda. "Because, apparently, Hesketh thinks the same thing."

Stephen stared at her, dumbfounded. "You're kidding me."

"No," said Brenda. "She seems to think she had you all wrong."

Casablanca

Lehmann Skye stood on his doorstep dressed in a 'thirties pin-striped double-breasted suit. He wore a wide emerald green tie with a golden airplane emblazoned on it. His hair was slicked back with goop that made it shine under the porch light. He grabbed Stephen firmly by the shoulders as if he had some pressing news to pass on to him. As if maybe Stephen's mother had phoned and told him he had to get right home. Then he spoke: "Why did you come to Casablanca, Rick?" He answered himself in a surly voice. "I came for the waters. But this is the desert. There are no waters. I was misinformed."

Lehmann laughed, and Stephen noticed he had a gold filling.

Lehmann had set up a machine that could project the image from a videocassette onto the wall of the Skyes' living room. He knew the film *Casablanca* by heart. He recited lines along with the characters on the screen or totally out of context, just as he pleased. "This gun is pointed right at your heart," he said. "That is my least vulnerable spot."

It was pretty distracting. Stephen didn't get all the story the first time through. He saw mostly the play of light and shadow, the urgency of the action, the love and pain in the faces of the actors. Humphrey Bogart was the guy in the trench coat, and the lead actress, who played Ilsa, was Ingrid Bergman. Stephen got that much. But the plot got jumbled up, and whole passages of dialogue were lost to him as party-goers wandered in and out of the room. "Here's lookin' at you, kid." That's what Lehmann said whenever Virginia tried to shush him up.

The film night was an excuse for Marlo, Virginia's mother, to try out some Moroccan recipes before including them in her catering repertoire.

Stephen liked Marlo Skye. She wasn't as glamorous or funny as Lehmann. She had a weary look, but her eyes were kind. And the food she had made was like nothing Stephen had ever seen or smelled or tasted before.

"She should have her name in the credits," he whispered to Virginia. "Exotic aromas by Marlo Skye."

The scents rising from the long table in the dining room mingled with the sense of the movie. Like music, the aromas colored everything.

There were spicy sausages baked in flaky phyllo dough; steaming round loaves of bread sprinkled with cumin and caraway seeds; big clay dishes of something called tagine of marinated lamb, stewed with prunes and apricots; a salad of sliced oranges sprinkled with powdered sugar and rosewater; a warm salad of green olives and coriander in a piquant dressing.

And cinnamon.

Stephen could still smell it on him when later, back home, he lay awake thinking about the evening. The laughter, the banter of the guests, the food—where did it all end and the film begin?

And everywhere was Lehmann Skye.

Brenda had once described Doug as flamboyant. Stephen had looked the word up in the dictionary because he had wondered what it might have to do with flames and staying afloat. It meant flashy and exuberant. The Ark— all that was really left of Doug in Stephen's life—was certainly flamboyant. Had he been like Lehmann, the life of the party? Did he laugh out loud, grab you by the shoulders? Stephen couldn't remember, and for the first time since his father left, it bothered him.

Joanna Carmody of the mauve biography and difficult birth was at the party. Her mother worked with Marlo sometimes, when she had a big catering job. Joanna herself had helped prepare the Moroccan feast.

Joanna had read a book about the making of *Casablanca* and kept spouting facts about who *almost* played the lead roles of Rick and Ilsa and how many writers were fired before the script worked out right. Stephen didn't want to hear. Didn't want to know that there were fights between the director and Bogart or how the movie was *supposed* to end. He didn't want to know that the actor playing Sam the piano man couldn't really play the piano.

Virginia had also invited a friend of hers from camp, named Ainsley, who lived in the city but came to stay over sometimes. She was a little morose, and tended to need a lot of Virginia's attention. She was always whispering to her. Stephen would strain to hear what she was saying and miss something on the screen.

And finally, Dom was there. Lehmann made a joke of trying to tempt him over to his high-school drama program.

"What's a good Catholic boy like you doing in that heathen school?" Lehmann demanded. Dom immediately launched into a song and dance about how he had been a maverick altar boy who burned down the cathedral in Buenos Aires and the Vatican was still on the lookout for him. The truth was that his mother was the head secretary at the school and wanted to keep an eye on him.

Virginia was thinking of casting Dom in a short movie. "Well, if you need someone short," said Stephen, "Dom's your man."

Dom had seen *Casablanca*. "Speaking of short actors, there's this amazing little guy named Peter Lorre. He plays this geek with saucer eyes and a nasally voice. 'Reek, you've got to help me!' " He grabbed Stephen's shirt front. " 'I have zis spicy sausage up my nose!' "

Stephen, it turned out, was the only person at the entire party who hadn't seen *Casablanca*.

"So, what'd you think?" Virginia asked him.

Stephen was eating a third helping of the tagine with saffron rice. "It's great!" he said.

Virginia took his plate away. "The *film*, Stephen."

"What film?"

Virginia frowned. "And here I thought you were the observant type."

Across the room, Lehmann, his tie wrapped around his forehead, was juggling an apple, an orange, and someone's red high-heel shoe. "Oh, I've been observing lots of stuff," said Stephen.

Virginia followed his gaze. "And me without my camera," she said. Stephen almost told her about her being in his dream, but it wasn't the time or place. Assuming there was a time or place you told a girl such a thing.

Virginia decided they would watch the movie again—just the kids—downstairs in the rec room, away from the adults. Stephen took along a plate of cinnamony cookies to help with the atmosphere.

This time he saw the film in a way he had never seen a film before. His eyes combed every shadow, every face in the busy marketplace, every corner of Rick's Café Americain, as if he were returning to the scene of a crime, some place where he might have lost something or left something behind.

"Maybe I did see this before," whispered Stephen.

"Then how could you forget it?" asked Virginia, bewildered. Then her eyes brightened. "Maybe it was something you watched through the stair rails when you were little and supposed to be in bed?"

"Maybe," said Stephen.

"Quiet in front!" yelled Dom, and Stephen sank back into the movie as if it were a dream.

"What do you think now?" Virginia asked Stephen, when it was all over for the second time and the lights were back on.

"Everything would have been fine for Rick and Ilsa if Victor hadn't shown up," he said.

"But then there wouldn't have been any *story*," said Virginia.

"What I want to know," said Dom, "is why only some of the cops have fezzes on. Did props run out of fezzes?"

The five of them sat at the bar in the Skyes' rec room

below the muted noise of the grown-ups upstairs. They were drinking fake champagne cocktails and ordering Ainsley, who was at the piano, to "Play it, Ainsley. You played it for her. You can play it for me." Ainsley picked out the melody of "As Time Goes By" with one finger.

Everybody drank champagne cocktails all the time in *Casablanca*. Virginia looked up the recipe in the bartender's guide. Soak a sugar cube with brandy and drop it into a glass of champagne.

They experimented. Once Marlo had ruled out brandy and champagne, they raided her huge kitchen for possible substitutes. Marlo wandered out onto the deck, a sweater over her shoulders. She was staring out at the night.

Probably exhausted, Stephen thought. He felt kind of exhausted himself and strangely sad.

"Hey, buck up," said Virginia. "It's just a movie."

Stephen shook his head. "No it's not," he said. "It's a film."

The best fake champagne cocktail was a sugar cube soaked in vanilla extract and dropped in Perrier. But they tried other stuff: almond extract, pear nectar, butterscotch syrup.

Dom even grabbed a bottle of something called *nam pla* from the fridge.

"That's fish gravy!" said Virginia.

"It looked like chocolate," said Dom.

"Hey," said Dom on their third round of drinks. "What we need is your medicine, Steve."

"What medicine?" Virginia asked.

"I have this problem," said Stephen, giving Dom the evil eye. "They don't know exactly what it is, but without the medicine I tend to make friends with flea-brained scumbags."

Dom turned up his collar and hoisted his cocktail. "Here's lookin' at you, kid."

Stephen held up his own drink. "Death to our enemies!" he said.

Upstairs the noise of the party rose and fell and Lehmann Skye's voice rode the waves of conversation like a proud schooner. When he laughed too loud or scored a resounding point in some debate, Virginia ground her teeth.

"Sometimes I just want to put an ad in the paper," she said. "One father, free to a good home."

Stephen frowned. "Whatever happened to 'If he left us, I don't know what I'd do'?"

Virginia stirred her cocktail with her finger until the last granule of sugar had disappeared. She looked at Stephen, and it was hard to tell from her eyes which was winning, the anger or the not showing it.

"Don't you think it's possible," she said, "to hate someone you love very, very much?"

Inside the Picture

It was like a scene from *Casablanca*. Everything was black and white. There were refugees everywhere escaping the Nazis. Every narrow street, every steep, stepped alley, every market square was thick with a moving flood of refugees.

Stephen was there. Doug and Brenda were leading him somewhere, holding him by the hand so tightly it hurt.

"Hurry up, Victor," said Brenda. "And stop wiggling."

"I'm not Victor," said Stephen, trying to squirm out of their grasp.

"What is it, sport?" said Doug.

Stephen kept glancing back. "We left something behind," he said.

"It's not safe here," said Brenda.

"We'll be rounded up," said Doug.

But Stephen struggled against his parents. Calling him Victor like that, as if everything was his fault! And besides, he had seen someone. It was Lehmann fighting his way through the crowd toward them.

With a mighty effort Stephen yanked himself free from his parents' grip and flattened himself against a wall to avoid being dragged under by the crowd. He looked back again, searching for Lehmann. But now he was nowhere in sight. The crowd pressed against him, crushing him. "Help!" he cried. "Mom, Dad." His parents were gone.

Someone grabbed him by the arm and pulled him out of the crowded street into a shadowy entranceway. He looked up into the shining face of Lehmann Skye. "Here's looking at you, kid," he said. His gold tooth glistened.

"How do we get out of here?" Stephen cried.

Then suddenly, all around him, the people stopped and stared at him. They threw up their arms and in their hands each and every immigrant waved a letter of transit. It was hard to get out without one. People would do anything for a letter of transit. Anything! The letters dazzled Stephen, fluttering like so many hungry seagulls over a swollen sea.

Sirens wailed like a league of crying babies, and instantly the streets cleared. Casablanca fell away. Lehmann was gone as quickly as he had appeared. In front of Stephen stretched a long meadow sloping down toward a distant forest. In a cleft in the trees he could see the last of the sun setting on the ocean.

A Volkswagen Beetle waited not far off, its nose toward the sea. As he watched, the driver's window rolled down.

"Doug!" said Stephen. "I found you again."

"Hop in," said Doug. "We've got you a letter of transit."

"What about the Something?" said Stephen. He turned and looked back toward where Casablanca had been. In its place was a grove of towering trees. There were houses in the trees all lit up. Tinkerpaw, backlit by a wall of flames. The sirens wailed again.

Doug looked anxiously in the rearview mirror and started up the engine. "It's the pigs," he said.

Brenda leaned over from the passenger's seat and smiled anxiously at Stephen. "We've got the baby right here," she said. In her arms was a little boy, fast asleep. "You see. You don't need to worry anymore."

The flames, by now, were licking at the massive trunks of the tree-house village. The sound of the sirens was growing louder.

"Climb on board, Stevie," said Doug.

"Please," said Brenda, reaching toward Stephen. "Let it go." Her eyes pleaded with him.

Sadly, Stephen shook his head.

Doug held up his finger to see which way the wind was blowing. "We can't wait any longer," he said, making some adjustments on his control panel.

Confused and sad, Stephen stepped away from the car. Immediately, Doug rolled up his window. The engine roared and the Volkswagen lurched away down the meadow.

Stephen stood watching them drive off into the gathering darkness until the car reached the end of the meadow, where it turned. He could see its headlights swing around to face him. It stopped. If he strained his ears he could hear the engine being revved up.

Then the Beetle was heading toward him, picking up speed. They were coming back for him—straight at him—but the car was going way too fast!

He felt numb, couldn't move. He looked down and his legs were rooted to the ground. He shielded his eyes from the headlights with his arms.

Then, suddenly, the lights weren't in his eyes any longer.

He looked up and the Volkswagen was rising from the ground, taking off. Stephen ducked as it passed overhead. He followed its progress as it climbed steeply over Tinker-paw, the flames briefly lighting its undercarriage.

"Cut!" cried a voice from down the meadow. It was Virginia. He could just make her out in the flickering light. She walked toward him, her eyes cast down. It seemed she was looking into the camera's viewfinder, reviewing the film she had just shot. She looked so cool, so unconcerned about the fire raging out of control nearby.

"Doesn't anything frighten you?" Stephen asked.

"It's not my dream," she said.

"It's not mine, either," shouted Stephen. "So why am I here?"

Virginia shrugged. "Because you have to find out what the Something is. Maybe it's in here."

She rewound the videotape. They bent their heads to review the footage she had taken. There was Lehmann, still trapped in the crowd, looking for Stephen, calling out his name. "Stephen? Where are you, Stevie?"

"Hey," said Virginia. "You can't have him, he's my father."

Stephen held the viewfinder closer. Any minute now he would see what it was he was looking for. But with a flash, the videotape burst into flames that leaped out of the viewfinder, burning his eyes.

Stephen lay perfectly still, awake now, but with his eyes still stinging and with the dream still pulsing through him, out of control. It was raining outside. The rain soothed him, helped put out the fire.

How could he ever record this? It was too much. Tinkerpaw and Casablanca, Doug and Brenda, Lehmann and Virginia, all jumbled up together.

The darkness softened around the edges. He concentrated, hardly daring to breathe, afraid that even breath might be enough to shatter the dream. It was as gossamer thin as a spider's web, and there was Stephen like a spider waiting for the tug of something caught in the finely woven trap. It was there. He could feel it. A clue.

Without turning on his lamp, Stephen climbed out of bed and went to the window. The sill was wet; so were the skirts of the curtains and the copper sculpture. He grasped the hoops in his hands. The crystal felt cold and real.

Becalmed, Stephen the spider crawled in his mind toward the thing that was caught in the web of his dream. Beyond all the action and transformations, there was something else. The meadow. The runway for Doug and Brenda's flight to freedom. Where had he seen that meadow before? Then it came to him.

At the door of his room he listened. The Ark was asleep. He made his way down the crooked hall, down the half-log steps, his hand on the sapling rail. A staircase Noah might have built in a bad dream.

Downstairs, he went directly to his mother's office. It was at the end of another crooked hallway just past the front entranceway. Here there were more steps, up to a low door curved at the top like something Bilbo Baggins might have carved at Bag End if he'd smoked too much Pipeweed.

The office door was closed. The sign said GO AWAY. He opened the door anyway and switched on the light. He stood dazed by the brightness.

Every horizontal surface in Brenda's office was piled high with manuscripts, research material, books and documents of one kind or another. Her desk was a disaster, but

Stephen cleared away enough of the mess to find what he was looking for: three framed photos, one of each of the children. He sat down in Brenda's swivel chair and gazed at the picture of Marcus.

He was little, maybe three or four. He wasn't wearing anything except a grin and a banjo. It was a real, grownup-sized banjo somebody must have strung over his shoulder for fun. Marcus was laughing and hitting the banjo with a stick, his long, hippie-child hair flying around his tanned face. The old family photo albums had all vanished years ago from the Fair household. Doug had taken them, just about the only thing he took. This was the only picture of Marcus left.

But it wasn't Marcus that captured Stephen's attention, now. He concentrated on the scene beyond the naked little boy. A long meadow sloping down to a distant forest, and through a cleft in the trees, the ocean.

There were no tree houses in the picture, but this was Tinkerpaw. It didn't say so anywhere, but Stephen suddenly knew. That ocean was the Pacific, and below that smudge of forest somewhere was Santa Cruz, California.

Stephen had never thought much about where the picture might have been taken. In any case, it was a portrait, not a landscape; Marcus filled most of the frame. There was nothing much in the photograph beyond the happy little banjo player, front and center. But in his dream Stephen had entered this unremarkable landscape and, turning around, had seen what was behind the photographer—what Marcus would have seen, if he hadn't been smiling like a madman at the very eye of the camera. The tree-house village where the nightmare was born. Stephen was certain of it.

He held the picture up close. There were three women

standing behind Marcus, a little way off, beside a smoking campfire. One of them had her back to the camera and was busy with the fire. The other was in profile and was drinking a cup of something. The third was facing the camera. She was skinny in a long granny dress and bare feet, her black hair long and luxurious. Her face was out of focus, but Stephen was pretty sure it was Brenda.

"Stephen?"

Stephen swung around, startled. Brenda was standing at the office door. Guiltily, he put the picture back down.

"What are you doing?"

Stephen stared at his mother. Her expression was alert, suspicious.

"Nothing."

She approached the desk and gathered up some correspondence that was lying there. Stephen had hardly noticed it. Now he did. One of the letters was the one from Nan.

"Are you asleep?" said Brenda, looking into his eyes.

He shook his head.

"Then please answer me. What are you doing?"

But Stephen was more interested in what she was doing. She was stuffing the letters, all higgledy-piggledy, into her filing cabinet.

"I was looking for something," said Stephen. He was stalling for time, but to his surprise, Brenda did not press him. She seemed to have other things on her mind. What, Stephen wondered, did Nan have to say that needed to be kept from him?

Brenda stoked up the fire in the living room. She sat Stephen in the rocker with a shawl around his shoulders and made him some Ovaltine. Then she sat in the chair on the other side of the hearth and regarded him with a kind of motherly concern that Stephen had hoped to avoid. She got up and crossed the room to the old wooden ice box that served as a liquor cabinet. Stephen watched her pour out a small glass of some vile cordial a friend had made out of chokecherries or huckleberries or something. She rejoined him.

At first he thought she was waiting for an explanation of what he had been up to. But the longer he kept silent, the more he wondered if there was something she wanted to tell him. It was not the first time he had noticed this lately.

"What's up?" he would ask her. "Nothing," she would answer.

He didn't feel like playing that game now. So there was silence. They swapped reassuring smiles that didn't bear scrutiny.

He leaned forward and poked at the embers with a stick of kindling. He hugged the shawl around him; the Ark was a drafty vessel.

You couldn't talk when you were trying to remember a dream—not so much as a word. Talking broke the spell. And there was so much to this one that was new. His father, for instance. Doug figured everywhere in the pages of Dreamcatcher that were dedicated to Marcus's dreams. He was always climbing up the ladder to rescue Marcus. But he was never in Stephen's dreams. His voice sometimes, calling or bickering, but never Doug himself.

Because he never wanted to be, thought Stephen. It was Lehmann who came after him. Then he thought of what Virginia had said to him in the dream. "You can't have him, he's my father."

The wind picked up outside, slinging rain at the windows. Stephen closed his eyes. The Ark might almost be at sea, for it seemed to toss on its moorings, forgetting it was land-bound. Then he heard the unmistakable plinking sound of water dripping from the skylight onto the broad leaves of the Indian rubber tree. As long as it rained now and then, the tree never needed watering. It was thriving, twice Stephen's height. In fact, there were plants placed strategically all over the house to receive the rain. It was as if Doug had always intended the Ark to spring a leak.

From the Brow of the Hill

The rain kept up, on and off, throughout Sunday. Stephen finished his homework only to avoid doing his chores. Then he did his chores only to avoid Brenda's wrath. She had stayed up drinking cordial long after he had gone back to bed and had woken up with quite a headache.

At four, she had to pick up Toni at a friend's house. As soon as the car was out of the driveway, Stephen went directly to her office. The filing cabinet was locked. He searched everywhere for the key, without success.

Brenda was hiding something from him.

As exhausted as he felt, he was too restless to stay put. He threw on an old poncho and gumboots and went out into the woods. It was cold, wintry again. There were even fat snowflakes mixed in with the rain. Spring was like that in Stephen's part of the world. You could sit out on a patio eating mango one day and three days later catch snowflakes on your tongue.

His boots were old and torn around the top, too big.

Doug's boots. A memory stirred. He remembered following those boots.

"Come on, Pooh. Today I'm going to teach you how to use a number five gouge."

Stephen shook off the memory. He didn't need this. What was Doug doing, barging in on his thought like this?

He galumphed along through the dead leaves, wished Dom was there. What good was Pooh without Piglet?

By their secret pond he helped himself to a cup of frosty-cold water. It cleared his head of Doug but not of Brenda. There she was, hiding something on him.

With a sick feeling Stephen remembered Marcus saying the same thing even after she had broken down and explained about Tinkerpaw. "She's hiding something on me," Marcus had said. Brenda had answered his accusations. "Paranoia," she claimed. "Sleep-deprived fantasy." And by then Marcus looked the part, his eyes sunken, his football-player frame caving in on him. He walked around punching things. There were still depressions on the monkey-cage walls made by his fists.

Was it just fantasy? Stephen sipped some water, tried to think straight.

At the highest point in the meadow there was a rocky outcropping. Standing at the top of it he could see Virginia's big white house. He had thought in a very Pooh-like way that maybe if he turned up on her doorstep right about supper time, a wet waif, he might get himself invited for a Sunday meal. A little smackerel of Moroccan leftovers, maybe.

Gazing down the meadow, he was pleased to see someone in the garden. It was Lehmann. Stephen was about to wave, when he checked the impulse. He leaned against the gnarled old crab-apple tree that grew there, at the brow of the hill, and watched.

Lehmann was slouching at the little round table on the patio, his long legs stretched out in front of him. He was wearing a leather jacket, but his feet were bare. The striped umbrella was still up but only offered incidental protection from the sleety rain. He didn't seem to care.

Stephen couldn't see his face but by the set of his shoulders he knew he was frowning, angry. He's worn out from battling those crowds in Casablanca, thought Stephen.

He wondered what Lehmann would think of being cast in his dream. For that matter, what would Virginia think? It was one thing for her to cast her father in a movie; quite another for Stephen to borrow him.

Lehmann shifted in his seat, dug his hands deeper into the pockets of his leather jacket. Suddenly Stephen knew something about him he hadn't known before. This was the culprit who had slammed the door in Virginia's *Me, Myself, and Why.*

The sliding door onto the deck opened, and Marlo appeared, her arms crossed on her chest. She seemed to be talking to Lehmann, or at least her head was turned in his direction. Lehmann didn't bother to return the attention. Eventually she gave up, the door closed.

Stephen remembered her the night before, standing out on the deck, her back to the party. He had thought she was just tired, then; now he wondered if maybe there was more to it.

After a moment, Lehmann picked up a glass that had been sitting in front of him on the table and held it out beyond the shelter of the umbrella until slowly, fat drop by fat drop, its amber contents were diluted with rainwater. Rainwater mixed with snow.

Stephen turned back toward home. It seemed he wasn't the only one who'd had a bad night. He felt a sense of dread growing in him. When he came to the dark part of the woods, he started to run, slipping the whole way on the muddy path, never looking sideways down at Mordor. But he heard its music, all the same. Cello music.

The Usual Suspects

The rain kept up all through Monday. Virginia took her videocam to school. She made people jump through hoops all day.

"Stephen. I want you to walk into the girls' washroom."

"I don't think so."

"Not all the way. Just inside the door. Ainsley will go ahead of you and warn anybody who's in there, okay?"

"And?"

"And then put this on and come back out." She handed him a mask of Freddy Kreuger.

Stephen looked at the mask and handed it back. "I'd just love to do this for you, but I've got nightmares of my own," he said.

"Come to think of it, you don't look so hot," she said.

"Thanks."

She eventually got Dom to do the scene. Dom would do anything. She got him to wear the hamburger-faced Freddy mask in the lineup in the cafeteria, as well. One of the janitors, a big hairy guy named Guido, kissed Dom right on his ugly, rubbery lips. That wasn't in Virginia's script, but she caught it all for posterity on tape.

She seemed nervy. Hyperactive. Outrageous. Maybe she had been like this all along and he had been too blind to notice. He wondered if maybe, apart from being beautiful and smart and creative and a superb athlete, she was totally bonkers.

Or maybe it was Ainsley. She had not returned to the city. She was even taking classes with Virginia. She was always whispering to her, holding her arm, her hand. There was no getting away from her.

"Do you think we could talk after school?" he asked Virginia. He wanted to ask her if things were okay at home. But it was Ainsley who answered. She had a kid's hand puppet, a cute, fuzzy bear that she kept in her pocket except when she wanted to talk to anyone. Thread Bear, she called him.

"Sure, Stevie-poo," said Thread in a squeaky high voice. "We're goin' out for coffee. Wanna come?"

"Sure," said Stephen. A date with a bear. Great.

They went to Papa Plato's: Virginia, Ainsley, Joanna, Stephen, and Derek. Derek was a senior. He drove them downtown, Virginia in the front, Stephen in the back with Joanna, Ainsley, and Thread Bear. Thread kept giving him little kisses. Stephen brushed the puppet off, trying to hear what Virginia and Derek were talking about. *Kiss.* Trying to figure out what their relationship was. *Kiss.* He wished Dom were there. He was going to join them later, said he was on a secret mission. Dom would have probably bitten Thread's nose off.

Virginia made them pose outside the restaurant, just at the edge of the blue awning, which bellied low, filled with rainwater. She herself stood out in the traffic. Cars beeped at her; she paid no attention. She was V.E. Skye, intrepid filmmaker.

"Now, Derek," Virginia commanded in her director's voice. "Reach up and poke the awning."

"So that it dumps on us, right?"

"Right," said Virginia, her eye pressed to the viewfinder of the videocam. "Okay, rolling."

To Stephen's surprise, Derek did what he was told. A deluge of freezing rainwater poured down on the heads of the actors, soaking them. The water sluiced down Stephen's collar.

"Cut!" said Virginia.

Everybody made a lot of indignant noises but their protests didn't seem real. It was as if it was just the kind of thing you had to expect when you were an actor. Was that all he was to Virginia? Stephen wondered. Part of the cast? Another extra?

He sneezed. She took him by the arm and shepherded him through Papa Plato's door. "Coffee's on me," she said.

Papa Plato's was steamy with pizza-oven warmth. They piled into a booth by the front window. The coffee arrived in thick white cups. Stephen didn't much like coffee. He loaded it up with sugar and cream, too much cream, so it hardly warmed him up at all. The rainwater coursed down his backbone and by capillary action slowly soaked into his underwear.

Virginia convinced Papa Plato to let Thread Bear help him take a pizza out of the oven while she filmed him. On Papa Plato's large hand, the puppet swore at the restaurant patrons in Greek.

Ainsley got all huffy when Virginia took her puppet friend. She shoved her hands deep into the pockets of her jacket. Stephen watched to see if she maybe had a spare. A king, maybe. He began to hum: "It's a wonderful day in the neighborhood." Ainsley glared at him.

Papa Plato played Virginia's fool. He even put on the Freddy Kreuger mask. Virginia laughed too hard, too long. Stephen felt miserable. He didn't belong here, wasn't cut out for playing a part in somebody else's comedy. He thought fondly of the William Gibson sci-fi he was reading at home. If he were there now he could be curled up by the fire in his sweats with a bowl of taco chips.

Virginia piled back into the booth. Stephen caught her eye, a glimpse of something there behind the blithe glee-fulness.

"Are you okay?" he asked.

She leaned across the table until her face filled his vision, until he had to back off in order not to go cross-eyed. "Are any of us okay?" she asked. Then she laughed, and her laughter was empty of anything like mirth.

Stephen would have made his exit right then if Dom hadn't arrived. There was a tap on the window. Looking up, he saw him standing under the awning in a brown fedora with a purple hatband. The hat was pulled low over his eyes. He wore a trench coat, the collar up, his hands deep in the pockets. Bogey in yellow sneakers.

He made his entrance.

"Ask me what my nationality is," he said. "Go on, ask."

"What are you talking about?" asked Stephen.

"It's a line from *Casablanca*," said Virginia. "What's your nationality, Dom?"

"I'm a drunk."

Joanna rolled her eyes, but she couldn't help grinning. Dom squeezed into the booth beside her and she pulled down the brim of his oversized fedora to cover his face. "Pretty good," she said.

Derek lit a cigarette. Dom immediately grabbed it out of his hand. He took a long drag on it as if he'd been smoking all his life.

"The problems of this world are not my department," he said. "I just want to run my bar."

Then, before Derek could stop him, he demolished the butt in an ashtray.

"Hey!" said Derek. "Easy on the props."

Virginia clapped, but she made no move to dig her videocam out of its case and record Dom's antics. She suddenly looked tired, all the director squeezed right out of her.

Stephen stared down at his tepid coffee. He had hardly touched it.

Joanna pressed closer to Stephen. She was trying to put some distance between herself and Dom. He refused to take off the trench coat.

"It's the new me," he said. "And it could be the new you!" He thumped the table with his fist and pointed at each of them in turn. "They've got three more trench coats at the Goodwill and another couple at Penny Lane. We could become an army. Call ourselves the Usual Suspects."

Virginia called the waitress over and ordered another round of coffee.

"I wonder about the usual suspects," she said. "I mean, the ones in *Casablanca* who get rounded up. Think of it. There's some guy having a nice quiet cup of tea and the cops bust in and drag him down to the cop shop."

"Probably most of them would have been asleep," said

Joanna. "Even suspects sleep—oh, I like that. 'Even Suspects Sleep.' " She looked as if she were seeing how well all the S's would look in calligraphy.

Dom rapped on the tabletop. *Knock, knock, knock.* " 'Open up, police.' 'What'd I do?' 'You're one of the people we usually arrest. So get your pants on, you're goin' downtown!' "

"Just like being a teenager," said Derek.

Everyone agreed.

"Suspicious by definition. The Usual Suspects, I like that."

"We could make a movie," said Virginia. "We could turn the gym into the *casbah*, with palm trees and snake charmers, and make all the ninth graders into refugees."

"We could make the football team into the Nazis," said Derek. "They'd like that."

"The stage could be Rick's," said Dom. "There's a piano there that looks like it's been through the Second World War."

Then someone suggested that the principal could play the head of the Gestapo and Ms. Kettle could play a cross-dressed captain of the French police.

Free from any fear that any of them would actually ever do anything about it, the idea of turning the whole school into *Casablanca* grew. And then it petered out. A rainy-day diversion.

It was muggy in Papa Plato's. Dom undid his coat. Everyone grew quiet. Whatever spark had been driving Virginia had vanished. She leaned her forehead against the window, staring out at the cars splashing by.

Ainsley had slipped Thread back onto her hand. She was pretending to tickle Stephen's ribs. Stephen reached out and grabbed the bear by the neck. "You wanna live, Thread?"

Thread nodded, made strangled noises. Stephen let go.

"Then tell me what's up with her," he demanded, jabbing his thumb in Virginia's direction.

Thread looked at Virginia, rubbed his eye with his fluffy paw. "Boo hoo," said the bear. "It's like Casablanca around her house these days."

"Dad spent last night dividing up the CDs," said Virginia.

Stephen was devastated. Struck dumb. He, Dom, Ainsley, and Virginia—only the four of them now—were trudging home, out of town along Lake Road. It was a long way. Out past the vet's, the seniors' home, the auction barn, the abandoned nursery. The rain was relentless. Stephen wondered if he had ever felt so cold.

The Skyes were splitting up.

"He already tried to divide up the books," said Virginia. "You should've heard them fighting over whose theater books were whose. Dad said he needed them—all of them. Theater was still his profession, in case anyone hadn't noticed. He said if Mom wanted half the theater books he'd take half her cookbooks. It was like that."

They slogged on, and Stephen thought about when his own father left. Took nothing with him but the photo albums. Took nothing with him but the past.

"Tell them what happened next, Ginny," said Ainsley. "When your folks were fighting."

A wicked smile briefly lit Virginia's face. "I got the videocam. 'Don't mind me,' I said. 'But maybe this'll be useful in court.' That shut them up." Her voice cracked.

The irony was that Ainsley had come out to stay with the Skyes while her mother tried working things out with a new boyfriend.

"And your dad?" This from Dom. "You can't stay with him?"

But Ainsley's dad didn't know she existed. He was just someone her mother had met at a rock festival.

Dom kicked at a stone, expertly lifting it on the ratty end of his yellow sneaker and into the torrent running through the weedy gutter. "We're all fatherless," he said.

"You've got a father," said Stephen.

"A stepfather," said Dom.

Stephen snorted. "He's been your father since you were six months old. And he's totally great."

"Okay, okay. But for argument's sake, we're all fatherless, right? I mean, Joanna's father lives in Seattle. And your dad, Stephen, he's off building windmills in the Yukon or whatever. Ainsley's dad is probably still at that rock concert. And now Virginia's father sounds like he's ditching her."

"Not *her*," said Stephen, angry at Dom's insensitivity. "He's not ditching Virginia."

"Yes, he is," yelled Virginia. "So you don't need to defend him."

Stephen was shocked into gloomy silence. His mood was not lost on Virginia; when she spoke again, her voice had lost its aggressive edge.

"My dad is wonderful," said Virginia. "It's not just him . . . Mom's half the problem . . . Work . . . Life . . ." Her voice trailed off. They were a solemn troop as they neared Dom's corner. Another stretch after that, it would be Ainsley and Virginia's turn. Finally, there would be only

Stephen, who lived farther out of town than anyone, out on the fringe of the woods where his father had parked the Ark before taking off.

Dom sank his head deep into his raised collar, pretended to dig out a cigarette from his breast pocket, light it, take a deep drag. "You see, cats and kittens? It's like I told ya. The Usual Suspects."

The Water Rises

Stephen was in bed with a cold for three days. Brenda pampered him with ginger ale and chicken soup. A cold was something she could cure.

"We're going to have to do something about this," she said. Mercifully, this time doing something meant nothing more nauseating than a few drops of Echinacea now and then in a tall glass of water. Echinacea smelled like locker-room socks, but Stephen took it without complaint, too weak to argue and glad enough to have Brenda mother him without calling in the troops.

The cold shielded from Brenda his increasingly melancholy state of mind. It had come on big time walking home in the rain, but he had caught the bug a day earlier on the brow of the hill.

Toni helped keep his spirits afloat. She was delighted to have a captive audience. After kindergarten in the morning, she was in and out of the monkey cage for the rest of the day, bringing him things to play with, taking away things he'd finished with or she wanted back.

They played some cards. Brenda even found the time for a few hands of nine-five-two. It was like old times. Toni won every hand. That was the trick—making sure Toni won. They had done the same to Stephen when he was young. One day, when he was six or seven, he'd suddenly caught on. "Hey, I want to lose, too!" he demanded. But Toni was still happy to win every time.

"You guys sure are lousy at nine-five-two," she said. Stephen and Brenda exchanged secret glances over their cards. It was good to see Brenda smiling, even if it was only a game.

The highlight of his confinement was Virginia's phone call to apologize for the drenching at Papa Plato's and the bummer walk home.

"It wasn't that," said Stephen. "I was kind of run down anyway."

"I'm sorry about yelling at you," she said.

"You didn't yell," he said. "And anyway, I deserved it." Then he asked her how things were at home.

"Like Casablanca," she said.

"Your dad still on the warpath?"

She hemmed and hawed—obviously he was in the room.

"What we need," said Stephen, "is a Usual Suspects' code."

"And a magic decoder ring," said Virginia.

"Hey, look at this, Steep," said Toni. "The pond is getting really fat." She was at his window, staring out at the drizzle. She dragged him to the window to see. And it was true. The pond at the foot of the garden had flooded the bank and was creeping up the lawn.

"Lucky the shed is a dinghy," said Toni, her nose pressed to the glass. The pond, rippled by the wind, was lapping at the shed's foundation. Stephen had never seen the water so high before.

"It's lucky we live in a boat," said Toni.

Stephen headed back toward the comfort of his bed. "It isn't really a boat," he said, climbing under the covers.

"I know that," said Toni. "It's an ark."

The pond rose so high, it seeped into Stephen's dreams. On the first night of his illness, Stephen dreamed that Lehmann was walking along the old railroad bed. The flood had risen up the embankment; it looked as if Lehmann were walking on water. He was calling.

"Stephen? Where are you, Stevie?"

Those exact words, over and over again.

The next night, Stephen found himself on the ladder to the impossibly high tree house. The baby was crying and he was going to see what was up, when suddenly he heard something below him. Glancing down, he saw Lehmann climbing the ladder. Below him waves were lapping against the tree trunk.

"I made this ladder and it won't hold you," said Stephen. That made Lehmann stop. He looked behind him, then up at Stephen.

"So I'm supposed to drown, or what?"

"You're not my father," said Stephen angrily.

"Oh, that's it," said Lehmann, smiling. Then, holding the ladder with only one hand, he reached up and tore off his face to reveal Doug Fair's face underneath.

Stephen was furious. "Go away!" he shouted. "You're too late!"

On the third night the dream progressed a step further. Stephen was sitting cross-legged in the dark—curled up small. He was on a raft. The whole world was under water now. It was kind of soothing, rocking him gently, but still the voices came to him.

"Stephen? Where are you, Stevie?"

Lehmann again. Who does he think he is? thought Stephen.

Then he heard Marcus, too. And Brenda.

"Please, Stevie, come back."

They were calling as if he were lost, but he knew exactly where he was. He was hiding. He hated them. All of them.

They wouldn't stop calling him. And the strange thing was, their voices seemed to be coming from beneath the water.

Good, he thought. They drowned.

But if they had drowned, how could they still be calling? Then he heard the baby crying, and he smiled to himself. The baby will drown them out.

But it didn't, not quite. Their voices still reached him; in fact, they seemed to be getting closer. Curiosity got the better of him. On his knees he crawled to the edge of the raft to see if he could see their faces floating below the surface.

To his shock he found he was not on a raft at all, but high in the air, on a platform in a tree. Down below him stretched the cockeyed ladder he could never seem to climb, though much of it was submerged by now as the water relentlessly climbed toward his roost.

His first feeling was one of elation. I'm in the tree house, he thought. I made it!

Then suddenly a head burst out of the water directly below him. Muscular hands grabbed onto the nearest rung of the ladder, and a man pulled himself up out of the flood. He shook his long hair out of his eyes. It was Lehmann. He looked around in every direction.

"I'm up here," cried Stephen. "I'm here, I'm here, I'm here."

Lehmann looked up, his face glistening wet and handsome. He smiled. "Don't you think it's about time you turned off the tears?" he said.

Alarmed, Stephen looked around him on the platform for the baby. It must be here, for its crying filled his ears. But it was nowhere to be seen. Then he realized Lehmann had been talking to him. He was the one who was crying.

"Stephen?"

"I can't stop," said Stephen, wrestling with strong arms which, from out of nowhere, had come to encircle him.

"Shhhh," said a voice much closer than the dream voices. It was Brenda. She wasn't a dream; she was holding him, tightly. "It's all right," she cooed. "It's all right."

Her face, cast in the half light that had followed her from the hall, was creased with pain.

"But I've got to put out the fire," he said.

Collapsing the Crystal

So now she knew. The nightmare was out of the bag. And, as if that wasn't bad enough, Hesketh phoned.

"I'm not seeing her," said Stephen. It was his first day back at school after his cold, and he was sitting at the kitchen table doing catch-up homework.

Brenda was slicing onions. She sliced them into smaller and smaller bits. "It won't be like last time," she said.

"I'm sleeping great," said Stephen. "I'm thinking of trying out for the varsity sleep team."

"Sleeping *well*," said Brenda, moving on to the celery. "So *well* that you wake up screaming? 'I'm here, I'm here, I'm here!' What's that all about?"

Stephen closed his books, closed his eyes. "It was a dream about Christopher Columbus," he said. "You just happened to arrive at the moment he waded ashore in the New World."

"Okay. And what about 'I've got to put out the fire'?"

Brenda shoveled the vegetables into the saucepan.

Stephen listened to the oil sizzle. He matched the sizzle in his voice.

"You promised me, Brenda, no more pokers and prodders."

"The fire, Stephen," she said. "I want to know about the fire."

"Okay, since you asked, I was dreaming about burning a witch at the stake. I wonder what that could mean?"

Brenda stirred and stirred.

"There won't be any more pokers and prodders," she said.

"Thanks."

"After Hesketh."

Stephen threw up his arms in despair.

"Hesketh is the last. It's just that she got it wrong the first time."

"You can say that again."

"And so does she. That's the point—she wants a chance to get it right."

Stephen finished off a Dr Pepper. It was tepid, sweet but no longer refreshing.

"Oh, I was as surprised as you were, Stephen, by her session here. It seemed such a sham. I didn't say anything about it at the time. I guess I was embarrassed. But believe me, there's more to her than meets the eye. When I was compiling that book on alternative health care for Cedar Press, over and over again people told me that she seemed to have a sixth sense."

"If she had any sense," said Stephen, "she'd stop bugging me."

Brenda opened a can of tomato paste, stirred it into the saucepan, but the heat was too high and the tomato splattered her blouse. She swore, turned down the flame, and turned to the sink to soak the stain. Her back was rigid with tension.

Stephen sighed, tried to reel in his temper. "Brenda, I'm dreaming my way through something. I can't explain it. But I don't want Hesketh or anyone else sticking her nose in right now. I'm a good dreamer. Just leave me alone, please."

Brenda turned, close to tears. "I can't," she said.

He stared at her for a long moment, saw the naked fear on her face.

"What is this really about?" he said.

Brenda leaned on the counter, her head bowed. She took a deep breath and turned the burner back up.

Stephen fought down a sick feeling. "Is there something I should know? Have you got cancer or something?" he asked, his voice shaky.

Brenda cast him a tender look. "No, no. It's nothing like that." She was biting her lip.

"Is there some guy?" he asked.

"Horror of horrors!" she said, a hint of a smile coloring her pale cheek.

"Then what?"

She glanced at him again and her eyes grew large. He could almost see an explanation start to form on her lips. Then, abruptly, she clamped her mouth shut.

He began to collect his books. He hadn't really expected to get any work done. He had joined her to be sociable, to try to convince her not to be overly concerned about last night. Obviously, he was too late.

"I'm glad you're going on that retreat."

Her expression became guarded. She diverted her eyes, started cutting up mushrooms. It was a stalemate. Stephen got up from the table, his books under his arm. He stopped at the kitchen door.

"If you expect Toni to eat that spaghetti sauce, you'd better go easy on the mushrooms," he said. Then he went up to his room.

He hadn't lied; he was on to something. The dreams were carrying him somewhere.

After entering the previous night's episode in Dreamcatcher, he had flipped back to the Marcus dreams and come upon the stick figure picture he had drawn of the trick cyclist carrying Marcus on her shoulders across a tightrope. Maybe sitting on a shrink's shoulders would be easier than going it alone. But Stephen was out on the tightrope all by himself right now. He was the crying baby. That was disturbing and yet a kind of victory; he had discovered it all by himself. He had no idea what it meant or where it might be leading him, but it was something. Another step forward. He could hold the dread at bay, the melancholy, too. But if anyone—*anyone*—stepped on the tightrope right now, he was sure he would fall.

When Toni had been sung to sleep, Brenda came to him. She sat on his bed. He was at his desk, on the cordless to Dom. Brenda showed no signs of leaving. He said goodbye.

"Guess what?" he said, swinging around in his chair, talking fast before she got in gear. "Dom is doing a kind of informal survey on fatherless kids, and Cindi Mullen rules."

"The Seven-Eleven Cindi Mullen?"

"That's her. We're making Cindi honorary president of our new organization, the Usual Suspects. We'll have the Cindi Mullen Oath of Fatherlessness."

Brenda raised an eyebrow.

"Her father was shot in the line of duty!"

"Shot?"

"Yeah. With a *horse tranquilizer.*" Stephen's eyes filled with devilish glee. "The stuff was called Rompen. Great name for a horse tranquilizer, eh? Mister Mullen—I mean *Doctor* Mullen; he was a vet—he was giving Rompen to this jittery stallion and it backed up on him so suddenly he ended up giving himself the injection *right in the heart.*"

Brenda stared at him, a grim smirk on her face. "The Oath of Fatherlessness?" she said. The cadence of her voice suggested that this was all very droll, but she hadn't come to hear about the Usual Suspects or veterinary homicide. She had other things on her mind. He had a pretty good idea what.

"I don't want to see Hesketh," he said. "Period."

Brenda bit her tongue. She reached out to touch his knee as if she didn't trust the air to transmit what she had to say. "It's your call," she said.

Stephen was caught off guard. His mother was stubborn; he had expected a long drawn-out argument. He was so relieved, he wanted to give her something. "If I change my mind," he said, "I'll let you know." There. It was the best present he could think of.

She patted his knee and rose to go. At the door she turned. "Just so you know. Hesketh seems to have had some kind of a premonition."

And then she was gone, leaving the door ajar in case he wanted to follow. He did. At his door he called after her.

"Thanks so much for the information, *Mom.*"

She stopped in her tracks, turned. "What's that supposed to mean?"

He didn't bother to answer. He shut the door quickly,

resisting the urge to slam it. He leaned hard against it, not wanting to talk anymore. He needn't have worried; she didn't return.

He kicked the leg of his bed. Kicked his chair. He had called her "Mom" to rub her the wrong way. And it had worked. As if "Mom" was some kind of derogatory remark.

He found himself shaking with rage. Rage at his mother's manipulation. Rage against her obsessive dread. Rage that there were Heskeths around ready—for a quick buck—to stoke the fires of her apprehension. Rage at the way the witch had looked into his eyes as if she could see things there.

He flicked off the light, stood in the darkness. He felt the tightrope swaying under him. And below it? Water. Deep and smothering. He was going crazy. She was driving him crazy.

He regained his balance, went to his window. The moon was lost behind an impenetrable curtain of rain-heavy clouds. He threw open the window. The wind probed inside his shirt with cold fingers.

He picked up the Genesa crystal, bounced it in his hands a couple of times as though it were a ball. Brenda's present was supposed to fill the room with healing life energy. It hadn't worked for Marcus. It sure wasn't working for him. He raised it with both hands above his head and hurled it with all his might out into the night. He watched the globe of copper hoops bounce—once, twice—and roll down the yard into darkness. He waited for something like thunder or whatever sound positive energy makes when it can't get cleansed or balanced anymore. He heard a great big nothing.

No. There was something. He heard the pond lapping. It was halfway up the back lawn.

The Covenant

The dinghy was scuppered. The floor of the shed was under enough water to float plastic flower pots and planter trays. It had always been hard for Stephen to imagine the family living there when they first moved east, but now it seemed impossible.

He had been a babe in arms. They had come from Vancouver soon after he was born. Doug was filled with dreams. They bought this land and camped on it until the land—if not God himself—spoke to Doug and they came to an agreement, a covenant between them. He built the Ark on a rise where a dead tree stood. Dead but not rotten, tall and relatively straight. He cleared all the brush and smaller trees around it, but he didn't cut down the tall tree. Instead he stripped the bark off it, varnished it, and built the house around it. He lopped off the lower branches, but the upper ones he trimmed to support an oddly shaped skylight. From the bridge, the topmost landing, you could look up between the varnished branches and through the skylight and see Brenda's flag. It was pretty tatty by now.

The family moved into the Ark when Stephen was two. So he had no recollections of living in the dinghy, no fond memories. It was now little more than a repository for broken things: limbless chairs, toothless garden tools, a swing-set arthritic with rust. There were chicken feeders from when Brenda had raised chickens and spools of electric fencing from when she'd kept goats. It was there that he deposited the broken Genesa crystal, he in his father's old boots, Dom in a bright yellow pair of Brenda's.

"What are you gonna do?" Dom asked.

"I guess I could ask somebody in Shop to weld it back together."

Dom rolled his eyes. "I mean about this."

There was already a fusty smell of mold and rot in the flooded shed.

"Oh, wait," said Dom. Bending down suddenly, he tugged with both hands at something under the water. With a big plopping noise he pretended to pull out a plug. "That should do it."

Stephen laughed. He had propped open the door and with a snow shovel started to push water out onto the sunken lawn. It flowed right back in. Dom clapped. Defeated, Stephen threw the shovel back into the corner.

"The water'll go down," said Dom.

Stephen didn't bother to nod. He was leaning against a cluttered worktable, his head bowed. Dom clicked his fingers in front of Stephen's face. Stephen brushed his hand away.

"The real thing is, what are you going to do about Brenda?"

Stephen glanced at Dom with a lost look on his face. "I don't know."

"Steep, it sounds to me like she's got more to hide than letters."

Stephen's forehead furrowed. "Last night I had the strangest feeling. When she was talking to me, I got the idea that she was frightened. Not for me, frightened *of* me."

Dom's eyes grew large, filled with terror. He started backing away, until with a fumbling hand he grabbed a broken chair and held it in front of him while he snapped an imaginary whip over Stephen's head.

Stephen broke up. Then Dom hurled the chair away with a horrible clatter. "Ahh, you don't scare me."

Stephen's gaze fell upon the crystal. The spheres were bent beyond repair. "I get the feeling she's close to breaking," he said. "And I can't help thinking it's my fault."

"Your fault how?"

"I don't know. Even in my dreams, it's my fault. Remember I told you the one where I was in Casablanca? They were dragging me out of there, and Brenda—I mean the dream Brenda—she called me Victor, like the guy in the movie who wrecks everything for Rick and Ilsa."

Dom looked baffled.

Stephen abandoned his explanation. "I don't understand it either," he said.

"Could you ask her?" said Dom.

Stephen scowled. "You try," he said, tossing the crystal into the corner.

Then Dom picked up a soggy cardboard box filled with junk and hurled it.

"Let's make us some noise!" shouted Dom.

And they did. Thunderous noise. The shed was soon a disaster area. Then Dom got it into his head that the dinghy was going down. He strapped a bicycle inner tube to his torso as if it were a life jacket and flung himself out the door, into the boot-high water covering the bottom end of the lawn.

"Man overboard," said Stephen, and dove after him. They splashed around like mad children, howling and tackling one another, and Stephen forgot himself and laughed himself sick.

It was unusually warm, so instead of heading back in, they took off down the logging path to see what shape their place in the woods was in. They stomped through every puddle.

It was cooler in the woods. They were soon quiet and shivering a bit, though not ready to turn back. That was when Dom told Stephen that their Easter plans had changed.

"We're still going to Tía Helena's, but my grandmother—my abuela—Rosa is coming from Buenos Aires. So it's going to be this big deal."

"Sounds cool," said Stephen, trying to hide his disappointment. He liked Dom's folks, had been looking forward to the trip to the city. The Amistades' very elastic sense of what constituted family had always stretched to include him if he happened to be around. He had met Tía Helena and Tío Jorge already, and they were a riot. But something in Dom's voice led him to believe that Abuela Rosa might be a different kettle of fish.

"She's all right," said Dom. "If you like Mass. My grandmother loves Mass. When she's here, we go to Mass a lot. But in between she spoils you rotten, so it is kind of cool."

"Mass," said Stephen, sinking from disappointment to desolation.

"Oh, you don't have to come," said Dom.

"Well, that's something, at least."

"In fact, Good Friday is going to be wall-to-wall church services."

"Just what I was hoping for," said Stephen.

"It's theater, you heathen. You get to roll around on the church floor, lamenting. Then you have to kiss the fish."

"Kiss the what?"

"The Good Friday fish."

"You're kidding me."

"Yep. But you still might want to find something to do on your own Good Friday."

That idea wasn't so bad. Stephen hardly ever got to the city. There were great record stores, neat places to hang out. If anything was open on Good Friday.

A strange noise suddenly caught their attention. They lifted their eyes skyward. Geese. A huge ragged V of Canada geese heading north. They each shot about thirty of them with sticks. Then Dom lobbed a couple of pinecone hand grenades to finish off the flock. It was thirsty-making work. But when they came to their room, they couldn't drink from the pool. It was under water, polluted with vegetable matter from the forest floor. The cup that hung from the tree was bobbing on the flood.

They headed back to the Ark for some lunch, seriously shivering now. Another flock of geese flew overhead. They let them pass in peace.

They changed and went back downstairs. Brenda was in her office with a deadline—Saturday was a luxury she couldn't afford.

"Can you guys make some lunch for yourselves and the girls?"

Toni and her friend Dee were playing in the living

room. They were using planks of wood, mailing tubes, blankets, and chairs.

"What are you building?" Stephen asked, lifting up one corner of a blanket. Toni slapped his hand.

"It's a fax machine," she said.

"Yeah? Looks like the rocket you built last week."

Toni shook her head. "Just shows what you know."

Dee put a sheet of paper under a slab of plywood and pressed down on it with her pudgy fingers. Toni pushed some "buttons" and shook the mailing tube that hung down from the contraption. A rolled-up piece of paper fell out of the mailing tube.

"Here's your fax," she said. She read the squiggly crayon lines. "It says the magazine article you wrote is great. We'll fax you your money right away."

Stephen and Dom cooked up a big bowlful of macaroni and cheese. Brenda had just joined them and was finishing off the leftovers when a van pulled up. A speedy rabbit with a parcel under its arm was painted on the side. The van was from the office supply store in town. They were delivering a real fax machine.

"See?" said Toni triumphantly. Stephen had heard nothing about his mother getting a fax machine.

The girls were disappointed by how small it was and quickly lost interest. Stephen and Dom watched the man install it. He faxed the store when he was finished, just to make sure everything was working right. The store faxed back a funny picture of the speedy rabbit on the logo looking like he'd been run over. Fax kill.

"Can I fax Virginia?" Stephen asked. He found Skye Catering in the phone book. The fax number was a separate line.

There was no heading to his letter, no salutation. Just "Here's faxing at you, kid." He and Dom waited around for an answer until Brenda shooed them out of the office.

This was obviously the one thing really wrong with a fax machine. The message had gone through, okay, but there was no way of knowing if there was anyone there to receive it. Stephen remembered the machine in Marlo's kitchen. A pizza maker, he had called it. Mr. Sense of Humor.

"The fax probably fell right into a vat of soup," he said.

"Cream of doubt soup," said Dom.

"Okay, so I'm nervous," said Stephen. "I've seen her with Derek a couple of times this week."

"They're working on some kind of project," said Dom. "Don't sweat it. Derek's cool."

Far too cool, thought Stephen. Leading-man cool. Way cooler than Stephen Fair, passive observer and all-around extra.

Dom had to leave midway through the afternoon. Then Brenda had to go into town before the post office closed. Stephen pleaded to go with her to pick up a movie—anything—just so he didn't have to wait around for the fax machine to ring. But he had to stay and watch Toni and Dee. He wandered into the office about every three minutes, swearing every time he saw the tray empty.

It was after five when he heard its distinctive ring, and he raced into the office to watch the transmission arrive. The paper, warm in his hands, curled slowly, slowly out of the machine, revealing—what? A magazine picture of a pizza.

Stephen was overcome with joy.

"She loves me," he said to the room at large, holding the fax to his heart.

Tiddlywinks

Easter was coming, but spring had stalled. The new leaves would not unfurl. There were strong winds from the north one day, from the west the next. Then an easterly would come swooping down, colder even than the north wind if you had to walk to school into the teeth of it. It was impossible to bicycle, but Stephen resisted taking the school bus. Virginia never did, as far he knew, and he hoped that if he could time his walk just right he might run into her. One day he did. But the wind seemed to snatch away every attempt at conversation—the very breath from their mouths as if even the elements were against him.

Another morning he arrived at the lake road in time to see Virginia speed by on the back of the Harley. She was holding on to her father for dear life.

The rain had stopped. But no one could stop the water rising inside Stephen. The question was how to stay afloat.

Virginia looked a bit washed out herself. Her father was

still around, but he had not unpacked the CDs. The boxes sat like a threat in the middle of his study floor.

"Midnight powwows?" said Stephen.

"Exactly. When I'm supposed to be asleep. As if anybody could sleep."

She had joined Stephen and Dom for lunch. She talked about her father's latest tantrum, her mother's turtle act, as she called it. Then suddenly she got all quiet. She went from vivacious to taciturn in the time it took to peel back the top of a peach yogurt and decide not to eat it.

Ainsley went home; her mother had dumped the new boyfriend. Not having Ainsley clinging to her arm or pinioned to her ear only seemed to allow Virginia more leeway for the blues.

Stephen couldn't do much about his own despondency, but he could try to cheer Virginia. One day after school, he showed up on her doorstep with butterscotch brownies he had made himself. She invited him in. She showed him the video footage she'd taken of them in the rain outside of Papa Plato's and of Thread Bear helping Papa Plato open the pizza oven. They ate the butterscotch brownies. The centers were gooey, undercooked.

"I had a dream about you," he blurted out. She looked amused. But he no sooner started telling her about it than he was interrupted by a deep-throated roar in the driveway. The hog had landed. Suddenly, Virginia got all hyper, chatting about anything and nothing, her eyes flitting toward the door. But her father, apparently, went around back to his study in the basement.

"What was it you were telling me?" she asked.

"Some other time," said Stephen.

He sent her a funny fax, a drawing of a lumpy field with someone jumping from lump to lump, wearing a big smile. The caption read "Every cow pat is an island of higher ground." It came back to Stephen with a P.S. from Marlo tagged onto the end of Virginia's reply: "Thanks for lighting up my day."

Stephen's own days needed lighting up. Brenda was increasingly difficult to talk to, hard to read. She said it was work. She spent more and more time hiding behind her GO AWAY sign.

At dinner one night Stephen mentioned that he might visit Nan over Easter when he was in the city. Brenda stared at him, her mouth gaping.

"Perhaps you didn't hear me right," said Stephen. "I *didn't* say 'I think I'll pump my veins full of crack cocaine over Easter.'"

Brenda stabbed at the food on her plate. "She hasn't exactly been communicative," she said.

"That's not true," said Stephen. "She wrote to you." The allegation hung in the air between Stephen and his mother, a challenge to which she refused to respond. "Oh, for cripes sake," said Stephen. "I saw this letter from Olive Place. What's the big secret? Is it something about Doug? What?"

Brenda seemed to relax a notch or two. She shook her head. "It's not about Doug. It's nothing for you to concern yourself with."

"Oh, good," said Stephen. "That makes me feel a whole lot better." He picked up his dinner things, dumped them in the sink, and headed from the kitchen, glaring at Brenda the whole time.

"Hey, Steep," said Toni, "there's lemming pie for dessert."

"Save me a piece," he said.

All the way to his room he thought of going back, confronting Brenda, insisting she level with him, while a little part of him kept wondering—if it's that bad, do you really want to know?

He sat on his bed waiting for her to come to his room. Maybe it was just that she didn't want Toni to hear. But she didn't show. Not even to say good night.

If his days were tense, his dreams seemed to have undergone some kind of mechanical breakdown. Almost the minute he fell asleep he was back in the tree house, but it was as if the nightmare was on Pause. Nothing happened. He was just sitting there waiting. For what? the platform to be whisked out from under him? He drew a picture in Dreamcatcher of himself sitting cross-legged in the middle of the air.

"Maybe I can't get down again," he wrote in the log. "Maybe I'm stuck up here forever."

He wished that he could talk to someone. He wished that he dare talk to Virginia. Or Lehmann. But things were up and down at the Skyes'. He didn't want to complicate matters.

Meanwhile, Brenda was watchful. His one night of screaming seemed to have confirmed her worst suspicions. He heard her sometimes in the hall outside the monkey-cage door, the dream patrol. He couldn't pretend anymore that his sleeplessness was anything as benign as a gnu on a treadmill.

She did not bring up Hesketh's premonition. She did not bring it up at breakfast. She did not bring it up at dinner. It was the most unmentioned thing in the Fair household.

"Okay, I'll see her!" he wanted to yell. "Just stop not mentioning it!"

But he resisted caving in. Brenda had given him the option of saying no. He needed to hang on to that little shred of power.

Stephen took part in only one extracurricular activity at school. Tiddlywinks. Specifically, the annual spring tiddlywinks showdown with the Catholic high school. For some reason he was good at tiddlywinks. It was a joke, really; a fundraiser that was built up as a serious crosstown rivalry.

The Big Wink-Off, as it was called, was held at the Catholic school that year. They alternated. Stephen's eyes searched the gym hoping to see Lehmann there, knowing, somehow, that tiddlywinks wasn't Lehmann's game.

He did run into him, however, in the hallway. Lehmann smiled at him and made as if to draw six-guns on him. "Eh, hombre," he said. "How do you do it? I hear you're the meanest winker east of the Rio Grande."

Stephen shrugged, as if his genius was still a mystery to him. "It's an eye thing," he said.

"You gotta make sure when you're winkin' not to blink, right?" said Lehmann. He laughed a great big punch of a laugh that made Stephen feel great.

"I guess you gotta watch the noddin', too?" Lehmann added.

"Oh, yeah," said Stephen. "Even with the winkin' and the blinkin' under control, the noddin' can kill ya."

Lehmann was still smiling, but he looked tired, his eyes bloodshot. Stephen didn't look much better himself.

"Haven't seen you around," said Lehmann.

Stephen smiled, tight-lipped, wishing there were something more he could say. Part of him wanted to say, "Why don't *you* come around? Why don't you unpack those CDs?" And another part of him simply wanted to say, "Is there room on the back of that hog of yours for me?"

But Lehmann didn't look as if he was going to tender any invitations. He looked all partied out.

The Letter of Transit

Then came the Monday before Easter. Only three days of school left.

"Holy Monday," Dom called it. He was practicing for Abuela.

"Have you got your lab report, Dom?"

"Holy Monday!"

"Look at the color of Boon's mohawk!"

"Holy Monday!"

Five P.M. The wind howling out of everywhere at once. The Ark creaked on its moorings. It was still light outside but with night and a full moon waiting impatiently in the wings, all their lines memorized.

Brenda called Stephen from her office. He was peeling potatoes for dinner.

"It's your fax-mate," she said. She was hard at work. The fax still lay in the bailer tray.

Stephen,

Don't know where to turn. Dad's gone berserk over a hair clip!!! He said it was on the dining room table three days. He said my hair things were everywhere. So he threw them all out. Clips, barrettes, elastics. Everything!!! We're prisoners here. He's taken the phone off the hook and I'm afraid to leave in case he hears me. He's holed up in his study. I don't think he'll do anything awful, but I'm scared. I'm hoping this gets through before he hears the machine. Help!!!

XOX
Ginia

Stephen looked at Brenda after he read the scribbled note. She didn't look up from her work. He guessed that she had not read beyond the salutation.

He went back to the kitchen. He sat at the kitchen table, his brain buzzing with berserk headlines. He cut himself with the kitchen knife. Sucking on his finger, he tried to shake the headlines from his mind. Lehmann wouldn't do anything awful. He had to believe that. But what was *Stephen* going to do?

Toni wandered in to see what was cooking. She was in high heels, with a pink boa over her shorts and T-shirt. She didn't speak, only filched a bag of crackers from the cupboard and left, dragging her boa behind her.

Maybe that's when the idea came to him. A vision jumped into his brain.

He had some phone calls to make.

Penny Lane Boutique was open until six. They still had the two trench coats Dom had seen there. Stephen asked the proprietor to hold both of them. Goodwill was just closing. He couldn't convince the saleslady to stay open even ten minutes. She had kids to get home to. He was pretty sure she didn't believe him when he told her it was a matter of life or death.

Then he phoned Dom. "I've got a job for the Usual Suspects," he said. It was coming to him as he spoke. A little play. Dom listened for his instructions.

Next Stephen turned his attention to the letter of transit. That was what it was all about. You had to talk to Lehmann in a way he could understand. Grab his attention. Everything was a play to Lehmann. Stephen wrote the letter, but it wasn't very good. It had to look and sound official.

He heard Brenda closing up shop. He took the letter of transit to her just as she was turning off the office lights.

"It's for a play we're doing in class," he said. "It has to sound like the real thing—you know, like a government thing . . ."

"A decree," said his mother, as she read his rough copy. "Hmmm." He saw her eyes light up. As tired as she was, the editor in her rose to the challenge.

"I'll do it on the computer in some pointy black-letter typeface," she said, flicking the lights back on.

"I'll finish making dinner," said Stephen.

Toni helped. He made her take off the boa, afraid it might catch fire.

"Your papers, *Mein Herr*," said Brenda, clicking her heels.

Stephen wiped his hands on his apron. The letter of

transit was great. Chillingly real. He gave her a big hug. "We've got a rehearsal tonight at Virginia's," he said.

"You do leave everything to the last minute," said Brenda. She held his chin in her hands and looked at his face. With her fingers she combed the hair off his face. "I hope this rehearsal isn't going to go too late," she said amiably. "You could just about pack those bags under your eyes."

Brenda took over the dinner preparations, while Stephen phoned around trying to round up the Suspects. Ainsley, of course, was back home in the city. Joanna had a test to study for.

"A test is more important than Virginia's life?"

"The idea sounds creepy," she said.

"It'll work!" Stephen protested. But Joanna wasn't convinced.

He sat biting his fingernails for a long time before he phoned Derek. He wasn't sure if there was anything between Derek and Virginia but, all things considered, it was Stephen she had turned to for help. Or was it just Stephen's fax machine? Anyway, what was more important: a rivalry he wasn't sure existed or his friend's safety? No question there. Besides, a car and a large senior seemed like a good idea. So he phoned, but Derek was at work.

Dom phoned back at five-forty, mission partially accomplished. He had bought one of the trench coats, the ratty one. The other was way too expensive. He had also been able to find another fedora.

"It looks like there's only us, anyway," said Stephen. "Are you still game?"

"We get to dress up, don't we?" said Dom.

But Stephen began to have serious doubts. He had

imagined a bunch of them delivering the letter: a dozen maybe, all dressed in the armor of costumes. And all of them, like Bogey, invincible, undeniable. Shock troops. He had imagined Lehmann impressed—stunned—by the performance.

Dom arrived just after supper. Brenda offered to drive them over to the Skyes', but Stephen said they wanted to walk.

They took the long way around to Meadowview Acres. The moon wasn't out yet and the woods were no place for a nighttime stroll.

"Sort of like Halloween," said Dom. "With no treats."

Only when they reached the Skyes' house did a sense of panic seize Stephen. There were few lights on inside. It didn't look at all welcoming.

"*Casa blanca,*" said Dom, pulling his fedora down over his eyes.

"Yeah, I know," said Stephen, a little testy. "It was my idea."

"No," said Dom. "I mean the house. *Casa blanca* means white house in Spanish."

For some reason that only made Stephen more nervous. "Maybe we should call the police," he said.

Dom recognized stage fright when he saw it. He elbowed Stephen in the chops. "Stick to the script," he said.

Clutching the rolled-up letter of transit in his pocket like a revolver, Stephen led the way around back.

"Oh, so we're breaking in?" said Dom.

"Virginia said he was holed up in his study."

The curtains were drawn across the study windows, but the lights were on. Stephen knocked on the door. He knocked again, harder.

The curtain opened. Lehmann was standing there.

The wind picked up and swirled around Stephen and Dom, the Usual Suspects in their Bogey gear. Stephen's teeth were chattering by now, but seeing Lehmann strengthened his resolve. There really was no turning back. Lehmann, however, didn't open the door. His eyes went out of focus as if he were looking down the barrel of a gun.

Stephen reached for the door handle. It wasn't locked. He slid the door open.

"Mr. Skye."

"What is it, guys?" The man's voice was tired, out of steam.

"We're here on business."

Lehmann teetered a bit, reached for the door frame for support.

"What kind of business?" he asked. His breath smelled of alcohol.

But before Stephen could answer, the door from the kitchen slid open and Virginia stepped out onto the deck above, Marlo one step behind her.

"Who's there?" she asked.

Lehmann stepped out onto the patio in his stocking feet. Stephen and Dom stepped aside. "It looks to me like a posse," said Lehmann.

Quickly, Stephen pulled the scroll from his pocket and thrust it at Lehmann. He had planned a little speech—like in the final scene of the movie: Rick at the airport, doing the noble thing—but it stuck in his throat.

"Stephen? Is that you?" Virginia was creeping down the stairway. Marlo flicked on the light over the deck.

Lehmann picked at the black ribbon that held the scroll closed. He opened the document.

"Letter of transit," Lehmann read out loud. Even in his condition, a bit of the ham came out in his rendition of the contents.

> The bearer of this document is hereby granted by the Authorities full right of passage within any sector of the territories overseen by this government, and the right to cross unimpeded into jurisdictions outside the power of this Authority. All border officials, armed forces personnel, police, or other persons charged with the duty of enforcing this government's laws and regulations are, hereby, through this document, instructed to let the bearer pass with all due speed and without unnecessary delay.

Virginia started to cry.

"What have you been telling people?" asked Lehmann, staring at her.

"She didn't have anything to do with it," said Stephen.

"I was frightened, Daddy," said Virginia.

Lehmann looked at the document, then at Stephen. "You're telling me I should get out of town?"

"Don't you get it?" said Stephen. "Like in *Casablanca*. You're treating your family as if this is some kind of a war zone." He couldn't go on.

Virginia was weeping freely now, which brought her mother quickly to her side.

"We don't want you to go, Dad," wailed Virginia.

Stephen had imagined only one scenario. Lehmann patting him on the shoulder, thanking him. "Phew! Thanks for bringing me to my senses, Stephen."

He had imagined Virginia throwing her arms around his neck, her hero. Now he felt adrift suddenly, as if he had been in the tow of a dream and someone had cut the line.

He gazed at Virginia sobbing on her mother's shoulder. He gazed at Lehmann sour with drink and hurt. He felt Dom prodding him from behind.

"Abort mission," muttered Dom. Stephen shook him off. Lehmann squinted at him.

"Oh, Daddy," Virginia sobbed. "I told Stephen you were acting weird. I told him I was scared. I'm sorry."

Dom was tugging on Stephen's sleeve. "Family time," he whispered. "Time to vamoose."

"I was just trying to help," said Stephen.

"You did, you did," whispered Dom. "Now come on."

But Stephen couldn't move. His head was spinning. Something was happening to him. He saw Virginia fling herself into her father's arms, he saw her father holding her, saw Marlo turn toward him and speak, but he couldn't hear anything anymore. No sound at all. As if someone had turned off the audio. Marlo reached out and touched his hand; he drew it back. He turned and fled.

He raced for the back fence, the gate, the meadow. Dimly he could hear voices calling after him.

"Stephen, Stevie, Steep. Come back."

But he wasn't going back. No way. They didn't understand; how could they? He was only trying to help and now look what he'd done.

Stephen ran with the wind behind him to the brow of the hill and then over it and down the meadow, the knee-high grass wet and sucking on his aching legs, slowing him down. He fell, tripping over the belt of his coat, tumbling forward into a juniper tree. He got up again, his hand scratched. He ran on, stumbling out onto the tractor path, his bleeding hand to his lips, tears streaming down his face.

He had lost his fedora; he didn't notice. He ran like a criminal, as if all the cops in Casablanca were hot on his heels.

He knew where he was heading. The moon would be his guide. It was where the dreams had been taking him before they had stalled. It was where he had gone when this had all happened the first time.

The Tree House

Doug and Brenda were arguing again. They were quiet enough about it. They never got loud; there were never any fisticuffs. It was a pow-wow. Once, when Stephen asked his mother what the difference was between a fight and a powwow, she said that a powwow was constructive. Now, as he listened, he wondered what they were constructing in there with words as sharp as trowels and as blunt as hammers.

"Don't say that," said Brenda. "I hate it. Anyway, you were there, too."

"And I was too much of a wimp to stop it. Say it. That's what you're thinking."

Marcus and Stephen stood at the master-bedroom door, in the vaulted alcove built around the dead tree.

"Come on," whispered Marcus. He had heard enough. He took Stephen's arm. But Stephen shook him off, bent his ear to the door.

"Of course I care!" Doug sounded hurt. "You think I don't care? It's just that there should have been . . ."

"Should have been what? An angel, perhaps?"

"It wasn't our right, Brenda."

"But it was right!"

There was a silence. Marcus tried again; Stephen wouldn't budge.

"We've gone over all of this a million times." Brenda's voice was barely audible. "We can't change what happened, Doug."

"And I can't live with it any longer," said Doug. His voice dropped, and Stephen pressed his ear closer to the door.

"I love him, Bren, but—"

Marcus yanked Stephen away. Stephen punched him.

"I'll make you a milkshake," Marcus whispered. Stephen punched him again. It was too late for milkshakes. Too late for powwows. It was time for action.

In the playroom there was a trunk full of dress-up stuff. That's where Stephen headed. He dug out the Roman centurion's costume that Nan had given him for Christmas when he was six or seven. He strapped it on over his pajamas. It hardly fit anymore—he was almost eleven—it was tight everywhere. A plastic breastplate, a helmet complete with cheek protectors, and greaves for his shins. There was a plastic sword, too, held together by electrical tape.

Armed, he climbed up to the bridge and threw open the door to his parents' bedroom. They laughed when they saw him—comic relief—but not for long.

He attacked Doug.

He whacked at him mercilessly with his plastic sword, howling at him, spinning away from his parents when they tried to grab him, writhing from their grasp when they tried to hold him. The tape on his sword gave way, the blade flopped over, tore off, but still he attacked, swinging wildly with his fists.

"I hate you, I hate you, I hate you," he cried.

Marcus came and watched from the door. Baby Toni woke up and filled the Ark with her wailing. Brenda had to go to her. Doug had Stephen in some kind of grip by then, but he broke free. He raced past Marcus, shoving him aside, making him spill his milkshake.

"Hey!"

He raced headlong down the spiral staircase, past Toni's room, down the front stairs, and into the mudroom, where he jammed his feet into sneakers still wet with a summer day's sweat. Before anyone could catch him he was out the door, down into the woods. Down into Mordor, where the Shadows lie.

It was a mild evening, a full moon, but in the deep woods there were shadows, all right. He had to make his way by feel, by heart. The underbrush closed in around him, grabbing at his bare ankles, clawing at his bare arms. Mosquitoes helped themselves to him.

He came, at last, to a clearing dominated by a massive oak tree, whose branches seemed to lunge out from every side like the tentacles of an octopus.

At the foot of the oak it was especially dark. He paused there, leaning against the trunk, patting it as though it were a trusty animal.

When he had his breath back, he climbed up steps nailed onto the living wood. There was a platform up there carpeted in leaf-patterned moonlight. There was no roof. No walls.

His heart slowed down, his hands stopped shaking. Around him the forest creaked with night life: the peepers in the swamp, the night-jars and nightingales, the hooting of a mouse-hunting owl. A breeze made the oak leaves tremble. And Stephen trembled, too, his centurion's armor no match for the night.

The memory rolled over Stephen. He leaned his burning cheek against the damp flank of the oak tree. He threw off his trench coat, unable to bear its weight another moment. The moon disappeared behind the clouds, plunging him back into darkness.

* * *

"Stephen. Where are you, Stevie?"

They were searching for him. He curled up small. Nobody at all knew about the tree house. Not even Marcus, although it was Marcus who had given him the idea to build it. In his dreams.

"Please, Stevie, come back."

They were up on the path to the meadow. They were walking the train bed. They were combing the bush, trying to flush him out. First just Doug and Marcus, then Brenda, too. But nobody would think to come down into Mordor. It was too scary a place, which is why he had built there in the first place. The tree house had to be his secret.

A frayed end of thick, yellow nylon rope hung near Stephen's hand. It was all that was left of his escape cable. He had been so proud of his escape cable. The rope had once been strung from the tree house to the base of another tree across the clearing. He could ride it down to the ground by hanging from a stout wooden handlebar suspended from a pulley. Stephen grabbed hold of the rope. He didn't remember it breaking. Had it just worn away with time?

Memories of that first nocturnal trip to the tree house rampaged through his senses. He felt the pain in his throat from all that yelling.

"I hate you, I hate you, I hate you!"

The risen Easter moon broke through the clouds, its light sifting down through the new growth springing from the branches above.

What had he been thinking? What he should have said—surely, what he'd meant to say—was "I love you, I love you, I love you." What had stopped him? Funny how you could get something so important so exactly wrong.

Stephen Dark

The gangplank leading up to the entranceway of the Ark was wide enough for two of every creature to climb. There were railings, in case you had been lost somewhere in the night for hours and weren't sure you had the strength to make it to the door. The door was hard to open. It swelled up when it rained too much.

Stephen heard folk music coming from the living room and wearily laid his head on his hands upon the newel post of the stairs. He wanted to go straight to bed, but Brenda would follow him. She would want to know where he had been, how the rehearsal had gone. So he summoned up what little energy he could and went to face the music.

He stopped before he reached her, just short of the soft light in which his mother waited up for him by the fire.

"Stephen, is that you?"

He pictured his father and Marcus in the woods calling for him. He pictured Lehmann, his hair streaming behind him, jacketless—his shirt filled with wind, flying low on some moonlit highway. He thought of how drunk

Lehmann had been and suddenly, in his mind's eye, the bike was out of control. He winced, clenched his fists.

"No," he replied. "No, it's not me." He wasn't sure she heard him. Didn't care. Because he wasn't Stephen Fair right now. He was Stephen Foul. No wonder his mother worried so much about him, wanted him cured.

This, then, was what the nightmares were about. This was the Something. The night he attacked his father and drove him away. And now he had done the same to Virginia's father. He had gotten it exactly wrong again.

He turned and headed for the stairs. He needed sleep to knit himself back together. In his despondency and fatigue, he was not a whole person anymore but only a collection of disconnected bits. A shadow of himself. Stephen Dark. He went to his room and fell into bed. Closing his eyes, he dared his nightmares to come and steal him away. But, not much to his surprise, even they steered clear.

Part Two ▾

Rock-a-Bye Baby

Stephen slept like a baby. He slept through breakfast. He slept through lunch. He was unaware of Brenda checking up on him, unaware of her hand on his forehead or taking his pulse. He awoke midafternoon more rested than he had been in months. Refreshed—exhilarated—he forgot, for several long minutes, what had happened, where he'd been. For several long minutes he was able to hold at bay the unexpected turn of events that had resulted in his discovery of the night before.

And then, when it did come back to him, it did not rock him as it had done last night. With thirteen hours of sleep under his belt, he felt he could deal with anything. Well, almost anything.

It was nearly two P.M. He tuned his clock radio to a local station for the top-of-the-hour news. There was no story of a fiery motorcycle accident involving a local drama teacher. He turned off the radio and lay with his head in his hands. As far as he knew, he hadn't driven Lehmann to his death. That was something.

If Brenda had heard about his theatrics at the Skyes', she didn't let on. But she was a wreck. It had been well after midnight when he got home. She had phoned the Skyes' a dozen times that night without success. "I'm glad to see *somebody* got some sleep," she said.

Stephen was afraid to phone Virginia. Afraid she hated him for what he had done. But he wasn't going to lose her friendship without a fight. He would fax her and try to explain. He sat down at his desk right after dinner. An hour later he hadn't gotten very far.

> Dear Virginia,
> I have made a big mistake! I am a dunce, a
> cretin, an imbecile.

Toni wandered into his room trailing the clean scent of baby shampoo. She was in her bathrobe and slippers. She hiked herself up onto his bed. "What are you doing?" she asked.

"I'm writing a letter to 'Ginia," said Stephen, without turning around. He read out loud what he had written so far.

"Does that mean you're sort of like an idiot?" she asked.

Stephen nodded. "Except I can't use idiot because it has an O in it."

"Oh," said Toni, in a matter-of-fact tone of voice. She could use the letter O any time she wanted. It was one of the letters she knew best because it was in her name, which was one of the words she could write.

"And because I can't use an O and there's only one R, I can't even say I'm sorry."

Toni brightened up. "You could borrow my O," she said. "And maybe I could get you an R from Mom."

Stephen smiled. He wondered what Toni would think of

his attempt to write Virginia an apology using only letters from her name. Probably that he was nuts. Probably she was right. He turned back to his task.

"Steep?" she said.

He grunted.

"Do you still have that medicine?"

Stephen turned to see his sister already moving around the stuff on his bedside table. Even as he watched, several books, including Dreamcatcher, and an empty mug clattered to the floor.

"Here it is!" cried Toni, holding up the vial Hesketh had given him.

"Hey, hold on," said Stephen. He went over and took the little bottle from her. It was still more than half full. "You know better than to mess around with medicine," he said.

Toni scrinched up her face and folded her arms crossly. "I need it for my dolls."

Stephen slipped the vial into his breast pocket and kneeled on the floor to clean up the mess.

"Please," said Toni.

Stephen sat down on the bed beside her. Toni crawled into his lap and began fishing for the bottle in his pocket. He wrestled her off; she was giggling mightily.

"But they need it," she said. "Especially Beach Party Barbie."

"Why?" he said. "Is she overstrained, full of dread, living in the past?"

"No, silly," said Toni, pushing him over and straddling him. "They're just jumpy." Stephen lay on his back, his arms flung out behind him. "It's been a tough day," said Toni.

Stephen had to agree.

"Couldn't I just give them a little smidgen?" she asked. "I've read to them—*three* stories—and I've tucked them in, but they won't go to sleep."

Stephen shook his head.

She punched him in the stomach. "Steep," she said. "Come on. You can get more from the witch-lady."

"No way," said Stephen, holding Toni's fist closed in his own. "That would mean I'd have to see her again."

"I know," said Toni, her face brightening. "That's why she's coming tomorrow."

Stephen raised himself up on his elbows eye to eye with his little sister. She immediately dove for his pocket and pulled out the bottle. He didn't try to stop her. Not quite believing her good luck, Toni scampered toward the bedroom door. When Stephen didn't pursue her, she stopped. "Aren't you going to chase me?"

"She's coming tomorrow?"

"Uh-huh," said Toni. "After school." She shuffled off to her room.

Stephen lay back on his bed, the weight of Toni's news pinning him down.

He heard Brenda on the stairs. He stiffened, sat up. In a flash he was at his desk again, a math book thrown open over his letter to Virginia.

"Hard at it?"

He didn't answer.

"Sorry to disturb you. I just wanted to ask if you would come straight home from school tomorrow. I have a meeting in town and Toni will need sitting."

"Right," said Stephen.

"What's that supposed to mean?"

"It's supposed to mean, right. Sure. Okay. Okay?" He

grinned brightly, but his eyes skittered away from making contact.

With an exhausted shake of her head, Brenda headed off to Toni's room. He waited breathlessly for her arrival there. Maybe she'd catch Toni feeding the sleeping potion to her dolls and come back to lecture him. Fine, he had a few things to say himself. Things about trust. Things about promises.

Stephen balled up his fist, then stared at it, uneasily. Maybe this was how you treated Stephen Dark. Tiptoeing around him, keeping secrets from him, never sure how he might react, who he might strike out at next.

His fist came down limply on his desktop. He made the sound of an explosion in his mouth.

He worked at the letter to Virginia for another hour, but the enthusiasm with which he had woken that morning had pretty well dissipated. Tomorrow kept crowding his thoughts.

"I have a meeting in town and Toni will need sitting."

No! Lying wasn't how you treated anyone. Why did she do that? What was she up to? He growled under his breath. Stephen Foul. Stephen Just Plain Fed Up.

At his door he listened to Brenda in Toni's room. Toni was pulling her just-a-few-minutes-more routine. Brenda was chuckling. They got along so easily. He found it hard to believe it had ever been like that between him and Brenda.

"I need to sing to them, Mommy. I need to sing my dollies to sleep."

Brenda acquiesced and, having secured Toni's promise that she would hop straight into bed once she was finished, left the room and made her way up to her own room.

Then Stephen heard Toni singing.

> Rock-a-bye baby, in the treetop.
> When the wind blows, the cradle will rock.
> When the bough breaks, the cradle will fall,
> And down will come baby, cradle and all.

And without knowing why, he started to cry.

Making the Blind See

The letter to Virginia didn't turn out so well. Without an O there could be no "you"; without a W there could be no "we." Her name contained no "apology." Nor could Stephen talk about there being any "excuse" for what he had done. Letter-wise, her name was twice the name his was, but still not enough to say the things he needed to say. He faxed it to her anyway, last thing Tuesday night, planning to fill in the blanks in person using all the words at his disposal.

Again he slept through the night, but his sleep was not dreamless. The tree house was there again, in vivid detail but empty. A still life, uninhabited, unremarkable. Not frightening any longer, only sad. Stephen awoke rested, thoughtful. He lay in bed remembering how Marcus had been after the revelation of Tinkerpaw. It explained some of his nightmare but not everything. Somehow Stephen knew the dream work was not over. It was as if he had made it on his trick cycle to a solid platform and now he was going to have to step off the platform, back onto the tightrope. To go where? And in the meantime, there was waking time to get through.

Once at school, he went straight to Virginia's locker.

"I am so angry!" she said when he tapped her on the shoulder.

"I can explain," he said. But before he could begin, she thrust a magazine in front of his nose and slapped the page.

"Look at this!" she said. "Just look!" Stephen didn't get a chance to look; she snatched the magazine back.

"I'm sorry," she said. "I wasn't thinking." And then she put her arms around him and gave him a huge hug. "Thank you so much," she said.

Stephen hung on to her the way a losing boxer clenches his opponent, not at all sure what's coming next.

When they separated, Virginia looked down at the magazine in her hands. "I just get caught up in issues," she said. She threw the magazine in her locker. "Forgive me?"

"Forgive *you*?"

"I'm so self-centered," she said.

"I guess it's going around," said Stephen, completely befuddled. But the fact that she was still the same old Virginia Elizabeth Dulcima Skye, ready to storm the battlements of advertising—or whatever it was—was better news than he had counted on.

The first bell rang. Virginia gathered together her books and closed her locker. "Mom and I are coping," she said. "We talked last night like we've never talked before. Dad's staying with a friend in town, but we've both been talking to him, as well. For an hour last night and before breakfast this morning. We're going to see a counselor together."

And then, before Stephen could say "Wow!" or "Great!" or anything at all, she grabbed him by the arm and started leading him down the hall. "Sorry about getting you mixed up in my family problems. Monday had just been the worst day, I kind of freaked out. But you were so . . . so brave."

"I was?"

"When you weren't at school yesterday, I wanted to fax you, but I was afraid. I felt like I'd gotten you into this huge mess. I wasn't even sure you would talk to me. I didn't see your fax until this morning."

"It wasn't much," said Stephen. "The fax, I mean."

Virginia was holding his hand, tightly now. "I was so worried," she said. She stopped and looked at him squarely in the face. "Here's me thinking you're the passive type. And here's you, Mister Man of Action."

Stephen blushed. But Virginia wasn't finished. "Of course, nobody's ever just one thing, are they? Nothing's ever just black and white."

"I guess you're right," said Stephen. "Some things are orange." He shielded himself, expecting a fist in the arm.

Virginia only grinned. "Some things *are* orange," she said.

She turned down the wing that led to her first class. He watched her, tongue-tied and transported. She turned around.

"I'm going to ask if I can film it," she called back to him, cupping her hand to raise her voice over the noise of the jammed hallway.

"Film what?"

"The counseling session."

Stephen was late for class, had to go for a late slip. He laughed all the way to the office.

* * *

It was the last day of school. Thursday was a teacher development day and then it was Good Friday. Stephen hoped to see Virginia again at lunch, but Dom dragged him downtown. In the dead end alley behind Papa Plato's there was an old auto shop that dealt in a few cars and bikes. Lehmann Skye's Harley was there, sitting out in the yard with a FOR SALE sign on it. Stephen looked for telltale dents, dried blood, but it looked clean as a whistle.

"I saw it down here yesterday," said Dom, as they stood staring at it. "What do you think we should do?"

"Do?"

"Do you think we should try to talk him out of it?"

Stephen shook his head in wonderment. "After what we did Monday, I'm just glad he's still alive. I had this picture of him crashing into a tractor trailer or something."

It was Dom's turn to look puzzled. "You don't know what happened? You should have returned my call." It seemed Dom had called the morning after their mission, but Stephen had been sleeping. "I guess Brenda forgot to tell you," he said.

Stephen didn't bother to comment.

Dom jumped on the bike. His feet didn't reach the ground.

"After you took off, Lehmann decided he needed a coffee. So we all went up to the kitchen and had coffee and some pie. Great pie. Key lime, I think—"

"Dom."

"Oh, yeah, well, Lehmann did a lot of apologizing for being creepy and said he needed some time to think. I kept trying to leave—it was family stuff—but they wouldn't let me. I was kind of like a referee. I wish I'd had a whistle and one of those cool black-and-white striped shirts—"

"Dom!"

"So about eleven, Lehmann phoned a pal of his who has an apartment downtown, packed a couple of things, and headed off. He was sober by then and gave me a ride home on the bike."

Dom's hands were wrapped around the handle grips. He made a revving noise.

Stephen stared at him. "You're making this up," he said.

Dom crossed his heart. "Why do you think I want to stop him from selling it, man? Just when we're starting to be friends? It's totally a rush. You've gotta try it. But you won't get a chance if it sells, *comprende*?"

He bent down low to the chassis in a racing stance. "Lehmann said your guerilla theater tactics—that's what he called them—were truly inspired. You called him on his Nazi act. That's how he put it. I bet *you* could convince him to keep the bike."

Stephen could not quite grasp it.

"You mean it worked?"

Dom threw his hands up in the air. "Yes, the stupid letter of transit thing actually worked."

Suddenly a mechanic appeared from the repair shop. "If you guys ain't purchasing that vehicle, buzz off!"

Dom said something in Spanish as he slipped off the Harley. It didn't sound to Stephen as if it had the word motorcycle in it. Then again, he was in a bit of a daze.

Virginia tracked him down between classes and asked if they could walk home together. Even the prospect of another confrontation with Hesketh couldn't dampen Stephen's spirits now.

She couldn't get over how effective the letter of transit performance piece had been. "It was like you'd known my dad all your life," she said, as they headed out Lake Road.

"I knew someone like him," he said. Something of Doug had come back to him. It was as if a door closed for so long was now open a crack and he could see Doug in there. His hair in braids, a red kerchief round his neck, a tool belt round his waist, clinging like a mountain climber to the side of the Ark, fitting a window. It was strange to talk about him, he'd shut this stuff inside for so long.

"He sounds cool."

"Flamboyant," said Stephen.

Then he told Virginia about that other night, four years earlier, that other performance, when he had dressed up and tried, in one last desperate ceremony, to get his own father's attention.

Virginia looked at him in wonder. "You couldn't save your own family from breaking up, but you were willing to take a big chance to save mine."

Was it really like that? Stephen couldn't say. "It just came to me."

"It wasn't your fault Doug went away," she said.

"I know that," said Stephen. He was trying hard to convince himself.

"The letter of transit thing worked on my dad because he really loves Mom and me." Then, with her hand flying to her mouth, Virginia apologized. "I didn't mean that the way it sounded."

"That my dad didn't love us?"

"It just came out that way."

"Don't worry about it."

"I love him, Bren, but . . ."

But what?

They walked in silence for a moment, but silence was the one thing Stephen didn't need. So he told Virginia more about Doug and about Marcus and Tinkerpaw and everything. He told her how Lehmann had come to him in his dream and helped to solve the mystery of the tree house in Mordor. He told her how she, Virginia, had helped, in her own way.

"What'd I do?" she asked.

"You filmed it."

"Wow!" She laughed. "This is V.E. Skye, on location in Stephen Fair's head."

They walked in silence for another stretch of time, a companionable silence. Stephen glanced at Virginia now and then. What was going on in her mind? She had that look on her face he had seen at school the day she'd been watching her video. As if she were seeing in her head what he had told her and was already twiddling knobs to make it come in better, brighter. Then she got a quizzical look on her face.

"Do you dream in color?" she asked.

"I don't know," said Stephen. But he recalled something the trick cyclist had told Marcus. He had written it down in Dreamcatcher because he found it unbelievably wonderful. "Apparently, even people who have been blind from birth still have vivid dreams," he said. "In dreams even the blind can see."

Under Hesketh's Spell

Hesketh's car was not in the driveway, not unless she'd disguised it with a spell to look like a trash can. Stephen checked for alien trash cans. He had tried to prepare for every eventuality, but out and out magic was beyond his control.

Brenda was in her study. He popped his head in to say hello, trying to act natural.

"Oh, good, you're home," she said.

"You bet," he said. "You can leave whenever you like."

She looked up, a pink flush coloring her face. "Oh, my meeting was canceled," she said. "Sorry. Hope you didn't have to change your plans?"

"Plans? Me?" He looked down. "I'll go see what Toni's up to."

Toni was up to her elbows in purple magic mud. She was at her own little table in the corner of the kitchen.

"Can you get the hair out of my mouth, Steep?" she asked. Obviously she had tried herself, for there was drying purple goop on her nose and cheek. Stephen cleared her hair out of the way and then washed the worst of the damage from her face with a washcloth. The rest would have to wait until her bath that night. She chattered to him, but he scarcely heard a thing. He was listening for the sound of a car.

"I'm just going to the bathroom," he said, trying to sound breezy. "I'll make us a snack when I get back."

He slipped into the mudroom en route. He looked out onto the driveway. No Hesketh. Maybe Toni had been wrong?

He had been careful, that morning, to tidy up some of the junk on the closet floor, enough so that he could slip in behind the coats without too much problem, but not enough that Brenda would notice. There was a removable panel, the size of a low door, on the back wall of the closet, held in place by four fasteners, all of which he had checked before school to make certain they were loose enough to turn. He turned them now and quietly pulled the panel away from the wall. Just in time. A car pulled into the driveway.

For a second he froze. It seemed so ridiculous, hiding in his own home. But then he clambered through the low entrance, banging his shoulder in the process, and dropped to the ground below. It was a low room, unfinished, filled with junk. Stephen could not quite stand up in it. Quickly and quietly, he maneuvered the panel back into place, plunging himself into darkness. Though he could not turn the fasteners from the inside, the panel fit snugly. He hoped it wouldn't fall out.

It was a crawl space under the raised part of the house that was Brenda's office. The Ark had no basement.

"What kind of an ark has a basement?" Doug had said. If the house really were an ark, thought Stephen, this would be where Noah housed the bugs.

It was pitch black at first, but gradually his eyes became accustomed to the dark, which was diminished by light filtering down through cracks between the floorboards of the office. He located the flashlight he had placed there before school. He bumped his head on a rafter, smothered a curse. Then he squatted on the floor, which was bare earth.

He heard the rollers of his mother's chair above his head. He was directly below her. He held his breath and listened.

Brenda answered the front door. It was Hesketh. He recognized the deep voice, the English accent. He heard Brenda hang Hesketh's coat. This was the moment of truth. If the coats swished against the panel, it might fall. There was nothing he could do to stop it. With relief he heard the women enter the front hall. Then Brenda called his name.

When she received no answer, he heard them retreat toward the kitchen. No doubt Brenda questioned Toni, for a moment later he heard his mother enter the front hallway again and walk toward the bathroom.

"Stephen?"

She called upstairs. "Honey? Where are you?"

She apologized to Hesketh, who had joined her in the hall. "I know he's home," said Brenda, heading up to his bedroom.

Hesketh stood in the hall, waiting. When Brenda returned, Hesketh said, "What's in here?"

Stephen went cold all over, waited for his hiding place to

be exposed. Then Brenda said, "My office. Would you like to see it?"

The stairs creaked beside Stephen's head. He looked up. He could just make out the underside of the flooring. It bristled with nails. Stephen ducked his head as if he had suddenly discovered he was in some casket of torture.

Hesketh asked Brenda about her work. Brenda answered distractedly. She obsessively apologized for Stephen's absence. "I didn't hear him leave," she said. "He must be in the house somewhere." Hesketh sounded only modestly concerned.

"I'll talk to Toni again," said Brenda, sounding both flustered and embarrassed. "It's been a challenging week."

Stephen's fists clenched. He almost pounded on the floorboards above in his anger. Then he glimpsed again the nails there and rubbed his fist, imagining the pain.

Hesketh did not follow Brenda from the office; only one pair of footsteps descended the little stairway. She stood maddeningly still so that Stephen was afraid to breathe. Then Brenda returned. "Toni thinks he may have gone to his place in the woods," she said. "This is so thoughtless of him."

"Not at all," said Hesketh. "It's spring. If I had a special place in the woods, that is where I would want to be on such a fine afternoon."

"It isn't far," said Brenda. "Care to come along? I can scare up an extra pair of boots."

"Thank you, but my hip has been acting up," said Hesketh. "You go ahead, dear, and I'll just wait here, if that's all right."

Stephen swore silently to himself. She didn't seem to be in any hurry this time around.

"Are you sure?" said Brenda.

Hesketh walked her to the mudroom. "I'll be fine," she said. Then the front door opened and shut and Brenda was gone. Hesketh wandered back to the kitchen. Stephen heard her speaking to Toni. Toni answered. At great length. Stephen could not hear what his sister was saying, but her voice had that singsong quality she adopted when she had a captive audience.

His legs were asleep; his feet tingled with needles and pins. He unfolded himself and stretched. Unable to stand the darkness another moment, he switched on the flashlight and beamed it around. It shone on Marcus's bunk bed. It gave him a start. He had forgotten it was here. There were a few other bits of furniture; otherwise the space was filled primarily with cardboard boxes piled on improvised shelves and skids. Old office papers: manuscripts, correspondence, income tax files. Most of it labeled. But not all.

Stephen's flashlight beam fell on an unmarked box that stood apart from the others, near the closet entranceway. He shuffled over to it on his butt and flipped open the top. Photo albums—five, six of them, and underneath a random assortment of loose snapshots.

He flipped one open. It was a family album. He hadn't seen the albums in years. Brenda had said that Doug had taken them.

Suddenly Stephen heard Hesketh's footsteps again. She was already entering the room above him before he thought to switch off the flashlight. Again he was in the dark.

She walked to the middle of the office floor, where she stopped and stood perfectly still. Then she did something that turned Stephen's blood to ice water.

"Stephen?" she said. It wasn't exactly a whisper, but subdued, confidential. "Are you there?"

Stephen held his breath so long he thought he might pass out. Then Hesketh spoke again in a forthright manner, as if there was much to tell and little time to tell it.

"I feel you are nearby, Stephen. I feel your distress. I was hoping to get a chance to speak to you alone. So this is fortuitous, though, admittedly, a bit strange. I am not used to communicating with the unseen."

She paused, but only long enough to catch her breath. "The way I work, Stephen, is to try to find blockages, energy impasses in the body caused by stress, emotional trauma, or physical injury. I thought I sensed that in you, but it was a garbled message. I have since had the opportunity to speak to Brenda a couple of times. I like your mother, Stephen. But I sense that she is the one suffering. I feel she is laboring under a weight of sadness well beyond a natural motherly concern for the well-being of an ailing child. Do you understand me so far?"

Below Hesketh, listening to her voice muted by oak floorboards, Stephen huddled in the dark, his eyes closed, nodding his head and rocking slightly in a kind of a trance.

"That first day, the feedback I got from your body confused me. There was so much interference. When I thought about it later, it was as if your body was a medium through which I was receiving conflicting reports. Then I remembered how your mother had hovered around, protectively, and a rather strange idea occurred to me, that my diagnosis—and therefore the prescription I recommended—was perhaps as much for her as it was for you.

"Do you remember what the flower essences were, what they were meant to remedy? That is why I loaned you my little book. That is why I hoped you would contact me.

You see, I think it is Brenda who is dwelling in the past and terrified that something awful is going to happen. Perhaps it is Brenda who feels she has something not quite clean about her.

"You see, the body is like a household, Stephen. There are blockages in this extraordinary household. This problem is something that I fear is coming to a head. I have not known Brenda long, but she is becoming increasingly disturbed.

"Has something happened recently, Stephen? Has there been some news that might have upset her?"

She waited as if expecting him to answer, but he could not speak. He only rocked in the darkness below her.

Hesketh moved. To the window, Stephen thought, to see if Brenda was coming. Then she sighed a long and weary sigh.

"What I think, Stephen, is that, unable to bear this grief herself—whatever it may be—Brenda has transferred it onto you. It is as if you have 'caught' her grief and it is magnifying whatever it is that causes your troubled sleep. She cannot heal herself, Stephen, so she is trying to nurse *you* back to health. She doesn't want you to suffer, but she is blind to the fact that her own unhappiness is the source of your suffering. Do you see what I'm getting at?"

Yes! thought Stephen, for as strange as it was, it made more sense than anything. Yes!

When Hesketh spoke again, her tone of voice had changed subtly, lost some of its urgency. As if she had actually heard him. It was an eerie thought.

"I had better go now. I shall leave a new prescription and a note on the dining-room table saying I have talked to you and that we may have made a breakthrough. You needn't fear the prescription. It is meant to work on

Brenda through you, a kind of sympathetic medicine. If she feels that you are getting better, it might help to relieve her suffering. In the meantime, the retreat this coming weekend will be useful to her, I hope. I have gone there myself in the past, and they are good people. When she returns, I shall try to find a way of getting Brenda to come and see me herself. Because nothing will be resolved while she holds to the idea that it is you who is sick."

At that point, Stephen heard Toni's pattering footsteps in the hallway. "Lady?" she called out. "Who are you talking to?"

Hesketh's voice dropped to a whisper. Stephen shuddered, for it was as if she were whispering directly through the floorboards.

"I don't like stooping to such subterfuge, Stephen. I hope you will understand that what I am doing is out of concern for your well-being, and Brenda's."

"Hey, here you are!" It was Toni's voice. She had skibbled up the stairs to the office. Stephen's strange encounter was over.

Toni led Hesketh back to the kitchen to show her something. Only a few minutes later, Hesketh left with cheery good-byes to Toni. As her car revved up, Stephen flung himself at the panel that blocked out the daylight and hurled himself up into the mudroom closet like a diver returning with empty scuba tanks from far too deep in the ocean. He leaned against the closet wall, gasping for breath.

"Schnitzel worms," said Toni. "And smushed bunnies and lettuce brains." It was what she wanted for supper, as usual.

Stephen shook his head. "Tacos," he countered.

"Can I grate the cheese?" Toni asked.

He nodded. "Once we clean you up properly."

While he was helping wash her hands, Stephen said, "Was it your idea to tell Brenda I was in the woods?"

Toni smiled her most mischievous smile. Stephen rolled his eyes in frank astonishment. Toni laughed merrily.

"I just wish you hadn't told the witch-lady where I was," he added.

Toni glared at him. "I didn't tell her."

Stephen scrubbed in stunned silence.

"Ow!" said Toni. "Not so rough."

They were hard at work when Brenda returned. Stephen mashed black beans steaming in the pot, listening to the quietness while she read the note Hesketh had left. Then Brenda peered into the kitchen, a perplexed look on her face. She held up the new vial of medicine questioningly.

"I think that might work okay," said Stephen optimistically.

Brenda's brow wrinkled. She looked harried. "Where were you?" she asked.

"Around," said Stephen.

Toni giggled. "Around," she said, covering her mouth with a cheesy hand, as if Stephen had made a joke.

Marcus

That night, when he had packed for the city and as soon as he could be reasonably sure that Brenda was not going to disturb him, Stephen pulled the dusty cardboard box of photo albums from under his bed.

This was one lie he could check up on. Obviously there was a reason she had wanted him to believe that Doug had taken the photo albums, something she didn't want him to see.

The first couple were of Doug and Brenda's odyssey around the continent. It began with a black-and-white eight-by-ten portrait: she with her lustrous raven hair down to the middle of her back; he fair-haired with braids. Stephen hadn't remembered until then just how blond his father had been, much more so than he. In fact, it was hard to find anything of himself in Doug's granny-sunglass eyes, striped bell bottoms, sheepskin vest, and polka-dot bandanna.

"Off to build new empires," someone had written in white ink as a caption.

The empires were everywhere: in woods and fields, by lakes and seas. Here was Doug, shirtless, his muscles bulging, digging a trench, shaping a log with an adze, poking his head through the tubular steel spiderweb of a geodesic dome. And here was Brenda, just as hard at work: laying tiles, weaving on a loom, maneuvering a wheelbarrow of wet cement down a wooden ramp.

Here they were on a farm in Prince Edward Island, in the hills of Tennessee. Here was Brenda pregnant with Marcus. And here was Marcus, alone, crawling naked through a worksite in the painted desert.

Stephen finished the first album, opened the second, looking for Tinkerpaw. And here it was. Extraordinary. How huge the trees were, how dense the grove. And the tree houses; they were not like anything Stephen had ever seen in real life, certainly nothing like his own tree house in Mordor. They were like something from a dream; a whole village halfway up the sky, linked by suspension bridges, tree to tree.

It was from here that his parents had fled to Canada, to Vancouver, where they had got their life together—that was a good one!—where he had been born the following fall.

He opened his eyes and gazed at the wondrous, tranquil settlement. He tried to imagine how such a place, in a single night, could have been turned into a nightmare. He imagined the open grounds beneath the trees crowded with visitors, musicians, bikers. He imagined fire out of control, licking at the trunks of the giant trees, climbing the rope ladders. He imagined his parents bundling Marcus up in a blanket, climbing down through the smoke, fighting their way through the crowds below to the Beetle, escaping across the meadow to freedom. Overland to avoid the cops. He shivered involuntarily to think of it.

Doug hated the cops. Pigs, he called them. Why? Were he and Brenda on the run? Were they drug dealers, thieves?

They had been crazy kids, his mother admitted. And maybe now she had a guilty conscience about something they had done in those crazy days. That seemed to be what Hesketh was implying. It was then he noticed that some pictures had been removed from the Tinkerpaw section. There were blanks on the black pages, the captions whited out.

The page was darker where the pictures had once been. A deeper darkness.

Stephen sat up straight in bed, in the grip of a chilling idea. What if someone from those days had tracked Brenda down and was blackmailing her. What if she was in danger! Could he help? Hardly. If she wanted to talk about this stuff, why had she hidden the albums in the first place, accusing Doug of taking them with him? What didn't she want Stephen to know?

Stephen was tired, his eyes sore. He had a crick in his neck and a low-grade ache in his heart. He was glad he was going away with Dom. He was glad Brenda was going to her retreat. Whatever was on her mind was taking her over; Hesketh was right about that. Dead right. It was she who needed help, not he.

He looked at his side table, at the bottle of remedy Hesketh had left him, meant to soothe not him but Brenda. He unscrewed the top, took a whiff, downed the whole thing. He lay back on his pillow and thought of that other remedy.

The cherry plum was for those who fear their mind is being over-strained, of reason giving way, of doing dreaded things. The aspen was for vague unknown fears of something terrible about to happen. The honeysuckle was for those who live in the past. The crab apple was for those who feel as if they have something not quite clean about them.

Oh, Brenda, he thought. What have you done?

He sat up to put the albums away. Stephen hadn't bothered with the loose photos at the bottom of the box, but he fingered through them now. And that was how he uncovered a snapshot brighter than the rest, of a face he recognized and yet didn't.

It was Marcus. He wouldn't have been sure if it had not said so on the back.

"Marcus looking macho in Martinique."

He was on some tropical beach in a muscle shirt, with the muscles to fill it. His father's muscles. He had a buzz cut and a ring through his eyebrow that glittered against his sun-tanned skin. There was a tattoo on his upper arm. A tattoo of a tree consumed in flames.

Stephen shuddered. It was his brother, all right, but it was no Marcus he had ever seen. There was a date printed on the back.

The picture was less than a year old.

Stephen's heart pounded in his rib cage like a prisoner rattling his cell door. Brenda was in contact with Marcus! Stephen was outraged. He wanted to go to her right then, wave the picture in her face, demand an explanation. He dug through the pictures and found another from the same roll, this one of Marcus and a girl, a redhead with pale, freckled skin, wearing a bikini, her face shaded by a huge sun hat.

"Me and Des. She's the pretty one," read the caption.

Stephen swore. He felt cheated. Deprived. Then suddenly, he felt nothing but faint, too weak to deal with any of this anymore. He didn't want to confront Brenda. He just wanted out.

He stared one last time at the photographs and the captions on the back. Despite his faintness, there was still one more shock waiting for him. The handwriting on the back—the handwriting that must belong to the person who wrote "Me and Des." He had seen it before. It was the same cramped "old-lady" handwriting on the letter from Forty Olive Place. It was Marcus who had written the letter to Brenda.

Marcus was living at Nan's.

The Mourning Dove

Bright and early Good Friday morning, Stephen Fair was delivered to Olive Place, a steep little cul-de-sac off Hillside Drive in a part of the city known as the mountain. It was not so much a mountain as it was a large and domineering hill. But it was a sheer enough climb that Tío Jorge put on his parking brake when he dropped Stephen at the curb in front of number forty. He wanted to go over with him for the twentieth time the bus routes back out to their home in the suburbs.

Dom sat in his Sunday clothes in the back of the van, squished between twin girl cousins in fluffy dresses, their braces glistening. He looked like he was going to a crucifixion. His own.

He reached over one fluffy-dressed cousin and rolled down the window. "Synchronize watches," he said. "It is now seven-fifty-three. We'll be back at the house by sixteen-thirty, sharp." The look in his eye said, "Be there."

Stephen synchronized his watch and crossed his heart.

"Say hello to your grandmother," said Dom.

"Okay," said Stephen, but this time he didn't cross his heart. He had lied to Dom and his uncle, said he had arranged to see Nan that morning. He hadn't told Dom of his discovery. He hadn't said anything to Brenda about finding the photographs, either. He was full to bursting with untold riches of secret information. It was a burden he didn't much enjoy.

He watched and waved as the van pulled a U-turn and trundled off down the hill, turned onto Hillside and, with one brief good-bye toot, disappeared from view.

He turned to look at his grandmother's house. He hadn't been there in several years, but nothing seemed to have changed. Like all the other houses marching up the west side of the street, it was neat and narrow, pointy roofed and reached by a stairway of many steps. Nan's garden was perhaps a little less tidy than her neighbors'. Unruly bushes encroached on either side of her stairway. Her steps were crumbling in places, and weeds had breached the cracked concrete here and there.

All the blinds and curtains were drawn. Nervously, Stephen climbed the stairway thinking of his brother, tanned and musclebound, with an eyebrow ring and that telltale tattoo. It was early; he wondered if it was a good idea to wake him.

There were so many steps; he reached the porch a bit out of breath but more from nerves than anything else.

There didn't seem to be a bell, though there was a recent-looking patch job where one might have been. He peered through a gap in the lace curtains on the window of the front door. Inside, there seemed to be a shared entranceway. This was new. He tried the front door; it was not locked. The vestibule was littered with shoes and rain boots of varying sizes. There were two doors, and on the wall two mailboxes: number one labeled S. FAIR; number two labeled M. FAIR. Stephen tried to remember his grandmother's name. Shiralee, that was it.

So Marcus was not only there, he had his own flat, a situation that filled Stephen with apprehension and more than a little hurt.

He plucked up his courage. There were two doorbells. Stephen tried number one. No answer. Number two, nothing. Finally he gave up and stepped outside, frustrated but vaguely relieved.

He would go for a walk, come back later. It was eight-twelve. It was going to be a long day.

He sat for a moment on the top step of the porch. The sun had just cleared the top of the hill and shone in his eyes. It was a beautiful morning, the wind fresh in the chestnut trees, the sky cloudless, the air warming. Perfect holiday weather. But Stephen's holiday prospects seemed anything but perfect now. Finding nobody at home at Olive Place had disappointed him more than he had expected. Why had Brenda kept Marcus to herself? Unless that was how Marcus wanted it. Was that why she was acting so weird?

I hate you, I hate you, I hate you.

The words reverberated through Stephen. Had he driven Marcus away, too? Try as he might, he could not recall the moment of Marcus's leaving. Had there been good-byes? A note? A scene? He couldn't remember.

Stephen sat, his chin in his hands. He wanted to see his brother. Guiltily, he had taken over his bed, imagined him dead. But sleeping in the upper bunk had never been the high he hoped it would be. He had learned to live without Marcus, to more or less forget him. But now . . . to know he was alive and yet not to be able to see him—it was too much. He still wore some of Marcus's old clothes. He still dreamed his brother's nightmares.

He would confront Brenda when he got home. He had hardly been able to look her in the eye Thursday morning. She had given him money for shopping on Saturday. He had barely thanked her, then slipped away from her hug to wait for the Amistades at the end of the driveway. Glancing back, he had seen her standing on the gangplank. She had waved and he had turned his head, pretending not to see.

So much for Hesketh's sympathetic healing.

A car turned off Hillside onto Olive Place. Stephen watched it climb slowly up the street to the circle at the end, where it turned and drove even more slowly back down, stopping in front of number forty. The two people in the car were too busy talking to notice Stephen, who was standing by then. He couldn't make out the passenger through the car's tinted glass, but she was old. She opened her door and stepped out. In the sunlight her hair blazed like white fire. Still talking to the driver, the woman opened the back door of the car and took out a small backpack, which she slung over her shoulder. She reached into the car again and very carefully lifted a brown paper bag with the top folded over neatly like a lunchbag.

Stephen was halfway down the steps by then. The driver spotted him and alerted the woman, who turned around, saw him, and gasped.

"Stephen?"

"Nan."

Despite her white hair, the woman before him looked anything but old. She was wearing white sneakers, jogging pants, and a bright red anorak over a thick sweater. She was trim and her hug, encumbered though it was by backpack and grocery bag, was hearty and welcoming.

"Bert, this is my other grandson, Stephen."

How long had it been since he had been introduced that way! A little overwhelmed, Stephen reached inside the car and shook hands with a middle-aged Asian man.

"Bert Ho," he said. "One of your grandmother's fellow Flappers." He burst out laughing at the look of surprise on Stephen's face. The noise made a grocery bag on the backseat jump.

They all noticed.

"It looks like *Colaptes auratus* may have woken up," said Nan.

"Two thumbs up for *Colaptes auratus*," said Bert. "Better get him to a doctor." He winked at Stephen. "Nice to meet you," he said.

Stephen said good-bye and closed the passenger door very carefully, his eyes still on the jumping bag.

"See you tomorrow, Bert," said Nan. He waved in his rearview mirror as he pulled away from the curb.

"It looks like your lunch has woken up, too," said Stephen, watching with some alarm as the sides of the paper bag in Nan's two-fisted grasp fluttered out.

Nan laughed. "Well, some members of the Columbidae family do make good eating, I'm told, but there isn't much meat on this fella."

She opened the bag just enough for Stephen to see the soft pinky-brown back of a bird—a live bird—with a long, pointed tail.

"It's a mourning dove," said Nan, closing the top again. "And I do believe it's time to set him free."

She handed Stephen her backpack and asked him to run it up to the porch. When he joined her again, they set off down the street.

"A remarkable morning," said Nan.

"You can say that again."

"Well, yes. Remarkable to see you after all these years. Remarkable for the sunshine—in my memory, Good Friday is always drab—and remarkable for Mister Mourning Dove," she said, holding up the bag. "In our species list we've only had a mourning dove once before."

"Why the bag?"

"Oh," said Nan, "we don't want to save a bird only to have it die of a heart attack. We like to keep our little customers safe and in the dark."

"You have a store for birds?"

Nan chuckled. "No, we Flappers don't keep birds, we rescue them, when we can."

"Flappers, huh?" said Stephen. He had heard of flappers. "Do you and Bert dance the Charleston and sing 'boop boop be do'?"

"Only when it's really cold," said Nan with a grin. Then she explained that she belonged to an organization called FLAP, a group of folks who went down to the financial district early every morning during the spring and fall migrations to collect the dead and injured birds who crashed into the skyscrapers. There were sometimes as many as a hundred a night. It was the lights in the office towers that disoriented the birds. That's what the Fatal Light Awareness Program was all about.

"And we had a very good morning."

"Were there lots?"

"Heavens, no! No. On the contrary, there were very few.

About six dead, and another dozen or so that need to be set free where they aren't likely to bump their heads again. That's where we're heading now."

They had turned up Hillside, where, ahead of them at the top of the hill, Stephen saw a boulevard of stately mansions and, across the street from the houses, a beautifully groomed park.

"Bert's going to drive that flicker to a bird sanctuary up-river. It broke its beak; maybe they can save it."

"Amazing," said Stephen. But he wasn't referring only to Bert's errand of mercy. They had reached the park, and it was like nowhere he had ever seen before. Sharply lit by the rising sun, it was like a green cathedral filled with wind music and stained-glass trees. The grounds were alive with dancing shadows and garden plots of rich black earth.

"This must seem tame to you," said Nan. "Living in the forest."

"The thing is," said Stephen, "in a forest you hardly ever notice the trees."

They were the only people there. The birds owned the place. They sang from every branch in a hundred tongues and with such fervor, it seemed they might lift the park clear off the hill and fly it away. On the dew-laden lawns the robins helped in the exercise, seeming to tug at the earth for all they were worth. Stephen laughed at the noise of it all.

Nan put the grocery bag down on a bench. Carefully, she opened it and took out the dove, cupping it in both hands. She held it, only for an instant, to her breast; then she set it down. The dove stood on the bench, its feathers stirred by the wind but otherwise motionless. It might have been a statue. Stephen squatted down to look it in the eye.

There was a light there, and fear. Maybe, thought Stephen, he was seeing in the bird's eye the memory of that light in the office window—the last thing the dove saw before it knew what hit it.

He reached out without thinking and gently touched the bird's wing. How warm it was, how soft. Then suddenly the dove exploded into flight, startling him. He fell over backward.

Nan laughed. So did Stephen, as she helped him up. They watched the bird land in the branches of a budding sapling on the other side of an empty fountain.

The dove cooed, a mournful sound but one that Nan evidently was glad to hear.

"Some of the Flappers drive all the way out of town before they let the birds go, but I'm pretty sure this is high enough. With any luck, our little friend is out of trouble now."

She sighed and sat on the park bench, folding up the bag and putting it in her pocket. "Quite a view, isn't it."

Below, the city glittered in the morning sun. Nan pointed to the skyscrapers of the financial district down along the waterfront. "What FLAP's trying to do is convince those fellas to turn their lights off at night. You'd think bankers would be interested in saving money, but you'd be amazed how much arm-twisting it takes to convince them of it."

"Look!" said Stephen. The dove had risen into the clear air and was wheeling high above them.

"Heading north," said Nan, her hands clasped in front of her face as if in prayer. "Clever bird."

"Right on," said Stephen, watching the dove wheel out of sight over a gray stone mansion.

"Maybe he's heading up your way." Nan looked at him then, as if seeing him for the first time. "My giddy godfathers," she said. "You're a teenager."

"Happens," said Stephen, smiling, a little embarrassed.

She looked at her watch. "I don't like to stereotype," she said. "But you're probably hungry, aren't you? Any teenager I've ever met had an empty leg."

Stephen shook his leg. "What do you know!"

"Good," said Nan, shaking her own leg. "Because I've been up since three, and I'm famished."

So Stephen waved good-bye and Nan cooed in passable Dovese to all the birds, the keepers of the park, and they set off down the hill toward Olive Place.

"So how about you, Stephen. Have you flown the coop?"

Stephen wasn't sure what she meant at first. "Oh," he said. "No. I'm just here for the weekend. Staying with a friend. Just a visit." Once he got started, the question seemed to need so much answering.

"Well, that's something," said Nan, looking relieved. "I thought maybe you were another refugee from the Ark."

"Refugee?"

"Oh, don't mind me," said Nan. "I'm prone to colorful language. I only meant there's been a bit of an exodus over the years, and I couldn't help wondering if you were the latest."

They walked in silence for a moment. Then Nan spoke again. "I never got along all that well with your mother, but all the same, it must be hard for her. How was she to know that feckless son of mine was going to leave her like that? Do you know what feckless means, Stephen?"

Stephen thought a bit. "I guess it means someone who doesn't have a whole lot of feck."

Nan laughed. "That about describes it."

They turned up Olive Place.

"Marcus was about your age when he left," said Nan.

"Exactly my age," said Stephen. "I'm glad he's okay. He is okay, isn't he?"

"I expect so," said Nan. "They're away for the long weekend. They're always flying off somewhere or other. I thought the baby would change all that—"

Stephen stopped in his tracks. "The what?"

Extra folds appeared in Nan's wrinkled forehead. "The baby. You don't know about little Ray?"

Stephen shook his head.

Nan's eyes brightened. "You're an uncle, Stephen."

Stephen's mouth hung open.

Nan closed it, gently. The brightness was still in her eyes, but it was tempered now with insight. "What else don't you know?"

Stephen's shoulders slumped. "I don't even know how much I don't know."

"Poor Stephen," said Nan. "You look as stunned as that poor dove."

Stephen nodded. "I guess you don't have a paper bag big enough for me, huh?"

"No," said Nan. "But I've got something better." Then she got behind him and pushed. "Come on. What we need is a pot of tea, a largish plate of cinnamon rolls, and a good long chat."

Olive Place

They sat in Nan's miniature kitchen. Nan put on the kettle and from her backpack took a small white baker's carton wrapped in string. It contained four fat, freshly baked cinnamon rolls, which she popped into the oven to warm up. In a matter of moments the fragrance transported Stephen back to far-off Casablanca. His thoughts drifted to Virginia. How far away she was. No, she was where she belonged; it was he, Stephen Fair, who was a long way away. And a long way from understanding what was going on.

Nan got him to bring in a chair from the sitting room, for her tiny polished table was only really big enough for one. In the center of the table, on a doily, sat a pair of bluebird salt and pepper shakers. Stephen fingered the china birds. They were warm in the sun pouring through the window.

Nan's flat was on the second floor. She had left the first floor for the kids; it was bigger and they could use the yard. By kids, she meant Marcus and Destiny.

Stephen wrinkled his nose. "Destiny?"

Nan's eyebrows did a little shimmy up her forehead. "I managed not to laugh, and you will show the same courtesy when you meet her," she said. "After all, she is your new sister-in-law. Or do you say out-law. They're not officially married."

Stephen pulled the two photographs from the breast pocket of his shirt.

Nan looked at them and smiled. "That's her, all right. She's a secretary for his band's recording company."

"Whoa, whoa, whoa!" said Stephen. "Band?"

"Savage Messiah."

"Marcus is in *Savage Messiah*!"

Nan nodded. "I gather they're big."

"They're huge! They're ginormous," said Stephen, but he frowned. "I've seen them on *Much Music,* and he isn't in the band."

Nan put her hand to her mouth. "Did I say 'in'? I guess I should have said 'with.' He started off as a bodyguard. Then he helped move equipment—a roadie, is that the word? And now he's learning how to 'run the board,' which I gather means he's some kind of a sound technician."

Stephen was shaking his head in disbelief. "Marcus works for Savage Messiah. Totally amazing."

Nan was looking at the photographs again. She appeared puzzled. "Destiny isn't really this plump." She turned the picture over. "Martinique. Was that before Costa Rica or after? Whenever he gets back from a long road trip, they go somewhere exotic. It's not that they have all that much money, but they have a good time. Can't keep track of all the places they get to." She examined the date on the photograph, counted on her fingers, smiled.

"Of course, this would have been when she was about four months pregnant."

She went on to tell Stephen how they had ended up at Olive Place. When the baby was born, their landlord had kicked them out. Marcus had asked her if there was any chance they could move in for a few weeks while he found a place.

"Well, the very last thing I wanted around was a couple of parents still wet behind the ears. But I had been considering dividing up the house. I don't have much pension, and an income property wasn't such a bad idea. I began to think of it as a kind of blessing in disguise. So, to make a long story short, I said yes. I had the place renovated *tout de suite,* and in they came."

Stephen stared at the picture again. "Destiny has a nice smile," he said.

"She's a good girl," said Nan. "Older than Marcus by a few years and sparky as all get-out. And heavens, he needed that."

Stephen was glad they weren't married. He didn't want to think he had missed a wedding. He'd already been left out of an awful lot.

Nan poured their tea. "What else can I tell you?" she asked.

"Tell me everything," said Stephen.

Nan took the cinnamon rolls from the oven, releasing their tantalizing aroma into the air. Her story came out slowly, with sweet interruptions until there was nothing left on the plate but crumbs and smears of icing, which Stephen cleaned up with an idle finger, listening—clinging—to every word.

"Marcus stayed with me on and off, a few days at a time,

when he first ran away. I was glad to help. I was worried sick for the boy; he was living on the street, in squats: an abandoned factory, a derelict carwash, an apartment building scheduled for demolition. He'd come here to crash, as he called it, get his laundry done, a couple of square meals in his belly, and then off he'd go. He has a lot of pride. It has kept him going.

"Eventually he got himself sorted out. He stayed at a hostel called Streets R Us. They treated him well, eventually offered him a part-time job doing chores and helping out with bouncing duties. I gather things sometimes got rough there on a Friday night."

The pictures were still on the table. Stephen stared at his brother's bouncer muscles.

"Oh, he's strong. So was his father."

Stephen flexed his arm without noticeable results.

"I daresay you'll put on some beef when you're a little older," she said. "Anyway, the bouncing led him to a job in a pub, which in turn led him to Savage Messiah."

"It's hard to believe," said Stephen. Nan looked annoyed.

"I find it hard to believe you haven't heard any of this before."

Stephen felt somehow a failure, unworthy of being taken into his mother's confidence.

Nan stared out the window at the backyard. He followed her gaze. It wasn't much of a yard, a few scattered items of plastic lawn furniture on a scrubby lawn, the beginnings of a sandbox in a corner.

"I know he wrote to Brenda," she said.

Stephen nodded. "He did. I never got a chance to read the letter, but I saw the envelope."

"Why has she kept it from you?"

Stephen shrugged.

"At first, of course, he wouldn't write. Refused. He had such a chip on his shoulder. I took it upon myself to phone Brenda." Nan looked uncomfortable.

"What happened?"

"Brenda was quite upset. Said I was stealing her boy. Seemed to think I was only phoning to rub it in. It was dreadful." Nan sighed, poured another cup of tea. "If I think about it now, I can understand. She must have been half crazy with worry. And I suppose she was still pretty resentful about Doug, too."

Stephen was embarrassed. "She isn't like that all the time," he said defensively.

"I'm sure she isn't," said Nan. "Whatever else I may have said, I admire Brenda very much." She sipped her tea thoughtfully. "But you know, she always seemed to me to take motherhood *too* seriously. As if she could never do enough for you, never love you enough."

Stephen flinched. Loved to death, he thought. "I guess Marcus got over it," he said.

"He mellowed," said Nan. "Then when Destiny got pregnant and Ray came along, he grew up pretty quickly. He talked about wanting to mend fences. They even went down, the three of them, to see your dad."

Stephen looked astonished. "Where?"

"New Mexico. He's got another family now, a baby not much older than Ray. He's building an adobe structure." Nan pursed her lips, thoughtfully. "For his new family's sake, I hope he doesn't finish it." She stared Stephen straight in the eye. "Know what I mean?"

Stephen figured he did. "Because he'll take off again?"

Nan nodded sadly. "That boy can build anything but a lasting relationship," she said.

"It isn't like that," said Stephen. His outburst surprised even himself. "I mean, he stayed with Brenda for over fifteen years."

The sad look on Nan's face softened. "It's big of you to say that, Stephen, considering how little he's done for you since he left."

Stephen slumped in his chair. "He didn't just leave to build stuff. There must have been other reasons."

Nan looked closely at Stephen. "Like what?"

Stephen shrugged. Me, he almost said. "I don't know." Then he looked hopefully at Nan. "But I'd like to find out."

Nan nodded. "I think that's what motivated Marcus to go and see him. He didn't talk to me about it when he got back, but he was more determined than ever to see Brenda. To see you all. That's why I don't understand about your being kept in the dark."

"Me neither," said Stephen. He grasped one of the china bluebirds and tapped it on the tabletop until Nan placed her hand over his to make him stop.

"Has he ever said anything about me?"

Nan leaned back in her chair cradling her nth cup of tea. She was thinking, and Stephen didn't want to watch in case her memory search came up empty.

"He once told me about a new song Savage Messiah is going to record. It's called 'Monkey Cage.' "

"That was our room," said Stephen. "In the Ark."

"That's what Marcus said. Apparently they were talking on the bus late, late one night after an engagement, and Marcus was telling the boys about the Ark and the monkey cage. The next thing he knew, they'd written a song about it. They're even going to credit Marcus on the record."

"Wow!" said Stephen. "That's so excellent."

"When he told me, I distinctly recall him saying, 'Wait until Steve hears about this. *He* was always the writer in our family.' "

Stephen felt a lump rising in his throat. Marcus had planned to tell him about the song. So what had gone wrong?

Suddenly, a cuckoo clock on the kitchen wall cuckooed ten times. Stephen almost jumped out of his skin. He pushed back his chair.

"What is it, Stephen? What's eating you?"

So he told her. About his nightmares and Brenda trying to heal him and getting so weird and almost spooky and what Hesketh had said to him and the incident at the tree house and how he really was beginning to think that if he wasn't crazy yet he was going to be if things around home didn't get back to normal soon.

"When was normal?" asked Nan.

The question caught Stephen off guard. How long had it been since Brenda was happy or at least acting ordinary?

"I guess everything was pretty good until some time last fall, around my birthday."

"October twelfth, isn't it?" said Nan.

Stephen nodded. "She was acting strange, kind of nervous, even before I had the first nightmare. That didn't happen until later in the month—I keep a log. Then they started coming regularly, 'most every night. I kept it from Brenda, more or less; told her I just couldn't sleep. But I was getting pretty run down. And that's when she started on me."

Nan nodded, but she looked thoughtful. "Are you

sure that's the way it was? Could it have been the other way around; Brenda's overreaction triggering the nightmares?"

Stephen was puzzled. But then, wasn't this sort of what Hesketh had been saying?

"I guess I'm asking you what made the nightmares start."

Stephen didn't know.

"You see, Ray was born in September and I'm almost positive Marcus wrote Brenda—maybe not right away—to pass on the good news. As I said, he did some real growing up once that kid came along. He's not much of a letter writer, I don't suppose. He sent those photos a year earlier, but I doubt that he wrote often."

Stephen moved to the wide arm of an old comfy chair, and sat down slowly, the wheels in his brain turning. "What are you saying?"

Nan held up her hands. "Nightmares may seem to come out of the blue, but I think they're usually set off by something. Just the way Marcus's were by your parents' breakup."

Stephen was beginning to grasp it. "You mean the letters. Brenda was getting letters from Marcus that she didn't want to tell me about."

"That's a pretty big thing to keep bottled up inside you," said Nan. "He wrote her again—I'm sure of it—when he got back from New Mexico. He really wanted to see her. He told me so himself."

Stephen was staring into the middle distance, listening and thinking. That would have been the letter he had seen, the one Toni had left in the rock garden. The one Brenda had been so quick to get out of his way that night in her office.

"Something he said might have spooked her. Some news about Doug, maybe."

The more Stephen thought about it, the more truth there seemed to be in what Nan was saying. Brenda had gotten progressively more ill at ease over the last month or two. He had felt certain she was hiding something from him.

Nan sighed. "She always was a jittery, impulsive girl. I'll tell you, Stephen, you're not the only one who gets nervous around Brenda. I hope for her sake and yours that this retreat does her some good."

Stephen's mind was racing, zipping around. The retreat. He thought back to yesterday morning. She had come into the monkey cage to make sure he had packed enough socks and underwear. He had been surly and uncommunicative.

She called him a few minutes later from Toni's room. Reluctantly, he had gone to her. Toni had been packing, too. She had just about packed her whole room. Brenda was exasperated. She wanted to know if Stephen had thought to get any money out of the bank for an emergency fund. He hadn't. She sent him up to the bridge to get some money from her purse. Fifty dollars. It was a lot; he had been surprised but not very gracious. How could he be, after finding those photos? The scene in her bedroom came back to him now in vivid detail. Her purse was lying on the middle of the bed. But now when he thought back, there was something conspicuously missing. Nowhere in her bedroom was there a suitcase.

"Stephen?"

He looked up, wide-eyed.

"What's up?" said Nan.

"Can I—may I—use your phone?" he asked.

She showed him to a desk in the front room and then left him alone.

"Please be in, please be in, please be in," he pleaded, as the phone at the other end of the line rang, twice, three times, was answered.

"Hi, it's me," he said. "Are you doing anything right now?"

The Ninth Hour

The bus terminal was Tiny's Gas & Grill. At three-twenty-one the bus pulled off old Highway Seven, into the gravel parking lot. It pulled away, and there was Virginia on the other side of the dust and exhaust. She was waving at him, sitting alone at a picnic table on a tiny patch of lawn outside Tiny's, sipping a soda. The videocam was sitting on the table.

She rolled the film she had taken and Stephen peered into the little viewfinder. She had phoned him back at Nan's to report what she had seen, but he was mesmerized none the less by the footage. It was the Ark, seen through the trees that bordered the logging trail. Brenda's car was in the driveway, as was another, a rental, by the look of it. And there was a woman, a redhead, out in the yard.

"That's Destiny," said Stephen.

"Cool name," said Virginia.

"Yeah, for a rocket ship."

Virginia had zoomed in. Destiny's hair was thin and windblown. Ray was in a Snugli on her front. She was patting the baby's back as she walked in a slow, rolling gait around the yard, obviously trying to get the baby to sleep. Stephen couldn't see anything of his nephew's head or face under his sun hat. But he could see his little fists waggling around outside the confinement of the Snugli, his chubby legs pedaling the air.

"And that's Ray," said Stephen.

Virginia grinned. "Do I call you Uncle Steve?"

Stephen didn't answer. He was too upset. Here he was, looking at his own nephew, and he felt like a spy.

Destiny's head turned toward the house. The camera followed her gaze; Marcus was standing at the door of the Ark, apparently calling to her. He waited, put his arm around her when she arrived, and bent down to give Ray's head a kiss. Then the door closed behind them.

Virginia zoomed in on the door. There was a time readout on the image. Eleven-twenty-six.

"Amazing," said Stephen. "When I asked you to go over there and snoop around, I didn't think you'd take your camera."

Virginia patted the camera. "It's how I see things," she said. She busied herself rewinding the videotape.

"It was great," he said. "Thanks."

Virginia clicked the camera lens shut. "We Usual Suspects have to hang together."

Marlo had dropped off Virginia but hadn't been able to wait, so Virginia and Stephen walked back to their end of town. It was a long way, but the weather was fine and Stephen wished this part of the journey would never end. He had no idea what awaited him at the Ark. Nan had wanted him to phone Brenda and let her know he was coming. He had refused, and he'd made Nan promise not to. Whatever was going to happen, it was going to be face to face.

Stephen filled in Virginia on what Nan had told him. He had not given her much in the way of detail over the phone.

"What are you going to do?" she asked.

Stephen shrugged. "I don't know. I'm going to play it by ear."

Virginia looked worried; it shook his confidence.

He had no plan, no armor. No Dom ready to wade into battle with him. Dom was up to his neck in Good Friday. His first duty that morning was to make hot cross buns. He had been enlisted by Tía Helena to help the nuns. After that he had to go to the church to walk the Stations of the Cross. It was a service, he had explained to Stephen, where you prayed all over the place, kneeling to meditate before pictures depicting episodes of Jesus's last day on Earth. It was as though you were walking the *Via Dolorosa,* the Painful Way, the route Jesus walked carrying his cross to The Big Hill.

Finally, there was to be a monster Mass in the afternoon at the hour when, traditionally, it was thought that Jesus had been crucified. Although the Mass was at three o'clock, it was called the ninth hour.

"How come it's the ninth hour?" Stephen had asked.

"How should I know? Maybe the Romans couldn't count. Maybe it was leap year."

There was only the one bus every day at two-oh-seven and there was no way Stephen was going to miss it. So he had left the city without even telling Dom, leaving Nan to phone him with his apologies and some kind of explanation. Stephen checked his watch. Three-forty-three P.M.

He wished he could talk to Dom himself: It's the ninth hour for me, too, pal, he thought.

He had no idea what to expect. Only that there was no more room for lies. All the secrets that had been locked away from him must now be released.

She loves us too much, he thought, recalling Nan's assessment of Brenda. He looked up into the clear, high, spring sky and took a deep breath of pine scented air. Pine, for those who suffer feelings of guilt.

Too much.

So much that she didn't hold any love back for herself. She didn't like herself—Hesketh had said as much, in a way. And that was so not fair.

Suddenly, Stephen knew something important. This was part of his anger. This frightened, self-hating, liar of a woman who had replaced his mother. He wanted Brenda back. Brenda of the midnight bowling alley. Brenda who knew how to lose at nine-five-two. The Brenda Toni knew and he had once known. Enough was enough.

Virginia elbowed Stephen gently in the chops. "A penny for your thoughts," she said.

"You can have 'em for free," he replied. They were pulling up to his driveway. She gave his hand a squeeze.

"I'll collect later," she said.

Stephen stood outside the door of the Ark, took a deep breath, and shoved his shoulder against it. It was still swollen from all the rain they'd been having lately; it still resisted him.

He stood in the mudroom, listening. There were voices in the kitchen. Companionable noises. They were having tea. It sounded homey.

Stephen slammed the door shut. The voices stopped.

"Who's that?" It was Brenda.

Stephen was going to say "It's only me," but the words stuck in his throat. With an effort he made his way to the kitchen.

There they were. Only baby Ray was missing. There was a plate of freshly baked cookies on the table. Stephen saw Marcus's face light up before both of the boys, almost simultaneously, turned to look at Brenda. She grated her chair backward across the floor. Her face was a portrait of agony.

"You're not supposed to be here!" she said. And then, looking as if she was going to be sick, she charged past him to the stairway that led past the dead tree to her bedroom on the bridge.

The Baby in the Tree

Stephen leaned against the door frame for a long time. Marcus spoke to him; he scarcely heard. At some point, Destiny passed him on her way up to look in on Brenda. She touched him on the shoulder as she went by. He flinched.

"You're not supposed to be here!"

Finally, he took a deep breath, and Marcus sat him down. He had gone to the living room for some brandy. He poured Stephen a shot, made him drink it straight.

The brandy in Hesketh's medicine had been watered down; straight, it was the vilest thing Stephen had ever tasted. He coughed, spit it up, and Marcus's big hand patted him on the back as if he were burping a baby.

"This stuff'll wake the dead," he said.

Stephen shook his head. "It sucks!"

Marcus chuckled. "Lukewarm tea more your speed, little bro?" He didn't wait for an answer but found a mug in the cupboard and filled it. "Milk, one large sugar. Right?"

Stephen looked up, happy for this stray memory. It was someplace to start.

"Welcome home," he said.

His brother's smile was shy. "Some homecoming."

"Yeah," said Stephen. "If I'd known you were coming, I'd have baked a cake."

Marcus nodded and tried to compose his face, but he looked awkward. Despite his broad shoulders and un-shaven chin—sitting down, now—he looked more like the kid Stephen had shared a room with.

"I've been wanting to see you a long time, Steve. This sneaking around—coming here while you're away—not my idea, man. Brenda has some stuff she needs to get through, that's all. She didn't want me to write you or any-thing. I said okay. Like I'm trying to play things her way. You understand?

Stephen looked down. He reached out and took one of the cookies. It was still warm. He took a bite. "Brenda's se-cret recipe," he said.

"Give me a break here, Steve. I want to do the right thing. I ran out on you guys. I don't want to screw up com-ing back."

Stephen put the cookie down. His mouth was too dry to eat. He swallowed a little tea. "It's not your fault," he said.

"She kept putting me off," said Marcus, his own voice bristling with frustration. "Finally I told her, 'Brenda, I want to make this connection. I want you guys to meet my family.' So we set this up to try and work it out."

"I get the picture," said Stephen.

Marcus cracked his knuckles one at a time. He looked preoccupied, but then he seemed to reach a decision. "But what you don't get is the big picture."

Stephen nodded. "That's what I'm afraid of."

Marcus took a deep breath. The cablelike muscles in his neck stood out like those of a weightlifter about to hoist a serious set of barbells.

"Remember when I was seeing the trick cyclist? Remember Brenda telling us about that tree-house place?"

"Tinkerpaw," said Stephen. "Yeah, I remember it, all right."

Marcus was about to go on, but he stopped himself and looked at Stephen inquisitively. "What do you mean, you remember it?"

"I mean, I remember hearing about it. Why are you looking at me like that?"

"Because the way you said it made me wonder if you, like, actually remember being there."

"How could I? I wasn't born yet."

Marcus leaned forward in his chair until his chin grazed the tabletop. His face was filled with discomfort. "That's just it, man. You were."

Stephen looked at him. "No, I wasn't," he said, but the words came out small, unsettled. "I was born in Vancouver the fall after Doug and Brenda *left* Tinkerpaw. My birthday's in October."

Marcus's eyelids drooped. "October's not your real birthday. They just chose it. It's more like February. Doug didn't know for sure. You're really about seven or eight months older than you think."

Stephen shook his head in disbelief. Then something Marcus had said made him turn cold. "What do you mean, Doug doesn't know *for sure* when I was born? He doesn't remember?"

The pained look on Marcus's face darkened. He couldn't speak. Then all of a sudden he looked up, past Stephen, and at the same moment Stephen swung around.

Brenda was standing at the kitchen entranceway. Neither of them had heard her return. She had left the kitchen looking grave; she had come back as quietly as a ghost.

"What Marcus is trying to tell you, Stephen, is that Doug doesn't know your birthdate any more than I do." She swallowed hard. "You were already born when we got to Tinkerpaw. You were there when we arrived."

Stephen couldn't look at her. He turned his head, looked at his brother instead.

"You're telling me I'm adopted?"

Marcus's eyes narrowed.

"Yes," said Brenda.

Then Marcus looked up at her, crossed his arms tightly on his chest. "No more games, Brenda," he said.

And Brenda said, "I'm getting to it."

Stephen couldn't stand the suspense. He jumped out of his chair and backed up against the counter, where he could see both of them. His eyes darted from Brenda to Marcus and back to Brenda. "Getting to what?"

Brenda's face contorted with pain. "We . . . we took you, Stephen."

The sentence meant nothing to Stephen. "Took me?"

"They kidnapped you, man. Doug and Brenda kidnapped you."

It was as if they were talking a foreign language, a language Stephen had studied in school, perhaps, but had never heard spoken out loud.

Brenda ventured one step into the room. Then she stopped. "We had to," she said.

"Had to?" Stephen's voice was slipping away on him, shrinking.

"We didn't mean to," said Brenda, her voice loud now,

plaintive. "You were in danger. There was no one to care for you. There should have been—"

Just then a baby started to cry. It caught Stephen off guard. It was back. The dream baby was back. He thought he had silenced it, but there it was, and it was outside of him as if it had broken through his skull and come into the real world.

"There should have been what? An angel, perhaps?"

"It wasn't our right, Brenda."

"But it was right."

"Stephen, are you okay?"

"It's just Ray, Steve. Baby Ray. Des'll see to him."

"We can't change what happened, Doug."

"And I can't live with it any longer. I love him, Bren, but he's not our child."

Stephen was at the door again—his parents' bedroom door. Marcus was tugging on him, trying to pull him away.

"He's not our child."

"Stephen, speak to me, please."

"He's not our child."

Now Stephen was breaking down the door and beating at his father. *"I hate you, I hate you, I hate you!"*

Brenda wrapped her arms around him. He pushed her off. He heard a door open upstairs. The crying stopped.

Stephen scratched with his fingernail at dried food trapped in the molding along the edge of the table. There was fresh tea now, hot and bracing. Marcus had been massaging his neck and shoulders, but now his strong hands rested lightly on the back of Stephen's chair. Brenda sat opposite him, her hands around her own cup of tea, looking up at him furtively, looking down again.

He was nodding his head like one of those little springy toy dogs people sometimes have in the rear window of their car. He had known this story for almost five years. He had just never known he was in it. The central character. The stolen boy.

"*. . . not our child.*"

He thought of the picture of Marcus in Brenda's office. The evidence was there. Why had he never seen it? There was Brenda watching her son play the banjo. It was supposedly the summer before Stephen was born and yet Brenda was thin, not a bulge in sight. She sure wasn't in the last stages of pregnancy.

He had wondered that morning how long she had been lying to him. Now he knew. She had been lying to him all his life.

"I had to, Stephen. I couldn't even pretend you were adopted. You'd want to know where and when and who your birth parents were. Doug and I managed to lie our way through getting you a birth certificate. Said we were living up in the mountains, that you were born naturally without even a midwife. That we didn't believe in bureaucracy, et cetera, et cetera. We lied and lied. I guess I just kept on doing it. Even to myself. I was frightened, afraid of what you'd do when you found out. When Marcus wrote last fall and said he wanted to see us, I kept it from you. I don't know why—the pictures, I guess. You two are so different. I don't know. Then when he wrote to say he had seen Doug. . . ."

Marcus's hands fell from Stephen's chair. He took a seat beside him. Stephen glanced at him, glanced back at Brenda.

"I don't know what to say, Stephen."

Stephen cleared his throat. "Just tell me the story," he said.

So she did. She told him about Yale and Sally, a couple that she and Doug hooked up with when they first arrived at Tinkerpaw. Marcus was almost four. Sally had just had a baby that winter; it was three or four months old. The baby's name was Stephen.

Brenda took to Stephen. Which was lucky, because neither Sally nor Yale seemed to have much time for baby-sitting.

"Marcus took to the ladder like a monkey—he was always athletic. But you were just at the stage of rolling over. I was afraid to take my eyes off you for a minute. I got into the habit of taking you with me everywhere. Yale and Sally didn't seem to mind."

"Hah!" said Marcus. "From what Doug told me, they were toasted most of the time."

"Then came the big summer solstice bash. It got so crowded; one of the tree houses collapsed. Nobody was hurt, but it scared me to death. I tried to convince your parents to move down onto the ground, at least until you were old enough to look after yourself. They figured I was after their house." Brenda's tone was laced with indignation. "They said nothing could happen to a baby in a place with such good karma." She couldn't go on.

"Doug told me they got real mad," said Marcus. "Said if she was going to go around bumming people out, they'd appreciate her finding her own place to crash. Can you believe that?"

Brenda, by now, had recovered. "I backed off. But I'd pretty well decided to be your guardian angel."

" 'An angel, perhaps,' " muttered Stephen.

"What?"

"Something I overheard," he said. "A long time ago." Brenda and Marcus exchanged glances. "You and Doug were fighting. I was listening at the door." Brenda turned ashen. "Please," said Stephen. "Don't stop now."

Brenda closed her eyes, tried to regain her composure, what little she had left. She took a deep breath. "There were bonfires and lights strung out everywhere. A lot of the people were strung out, too. The night got wilder and wilder. One or two fires got out of control. The Choice arrived—bikers. There were fights. I never budged from the tree house. I was like a bird on the nest; I wasn't leaving you boys for a second. Marcus was so angry; he wanted to party. I wouldn't let him. Finally, you both fell asleep. Then, sometime after midnight, Doug came up, really worried. There were rumors of a narc, an undercover cop. There was a lot of dope and Doug was afraid of a police raid. He didn't have a work visa. We weren't even supposed to be in the States; we were illegal aliens. He wanted to split right away. Thank God, I thought. So while he woke Marcus and got him dressed, I got you ready, Stephen."

She paused to make sure Stephen understood.

"Doug hadn't counted on that. 'We can't take the baby,' he told me. So I just sat right down again. You were crying by then."

"I guess that's what I was remembering in my nightmares," said Marcus. "I mean, all this stuff was going on, but it wasn't me who was doing the crying."

"It was me," said Stephen, as if, somehow, he had always known it.

"By then Doug was truly scared, so we headed out, baby and all. We got in the Beetle and floored it—cross-country so we wouldn't run into the cops. There was only one road to Tinkerpaw and they were on it."

"Doug figured we'd go back when things cooled down," said Marcus.

"And we did, a couple of days later." Again Brenda paused. "We went back, Stephen."

"It was some scene, I guess, the way Doug described it," said Marcus. "The fire had burned off some of the woodland, and the rancher who'd let the hippies use the spot was royally pissed off."

With downcast eyes, Brenda acknowledged Doug's version of the events. "The rancher was shutting the place down. Everyone was packing up their stuff. We looked in vain for Yale and Sally. Somebody said they had been busted. Somebody else said they just split. Nobody knew for sure where they'd gone."

Brenda reached across the table toward Stephen's hand. He pulled it out of reach. "We tried, Stephen." Slowly, Brenda drew back her own hand, which fell to her lap. "We didn't know what to do. Doug wanted to leave you with some folks there. Folks who knew Yale and Sally a bit."

"But you wouldn't do it, right, Bren? That's what Doug said."

"How could I? They didn't know your parents that well. Didn't know where they were going or even where they were from. And besides, they weren't into it. You think I couldn't tell?"

She appealed to Stephen, but he didn't know what to think.

"Do you think I would leave you with just anyone?"

Brenda fixed him with her eyes, pleaded for a response, some kind of sign. Would she have left him with just anyone? No. That much he felt sure of. He shook his head. It was acknowledgment, not approval, but it was something, at least. She could go on.

"So we left. Came home. Started a new life."

Upstairs in the Ark, a door opened. The threesome around the table looked up in anticipation. There were footsteps on the stairs.

The Namesake

Baby Ray rode into the kitchen in a clean diaper and a WHAT ME WORRY T-shirt, astride his mother's slim and freckled arm. His own talcum-pale arms reached out immediately for his father, who swept him up, pressing his mouth to the baby's belly and disturbing a flock of giggles that flew up into the still and melancholy air.

Destiny turned to Stephen, her blue eyes all sympathy. "How you doing?" She was holding out her hand in friendship. He stood up. They shook hands. Then Stephen got the feeling that she was thinking about giving him a hug, so he backed off.

Ray was now camped comfortably on Marcus's broad chest.

"Here, you hold him," said Marcus to Stephen. "Go on."

Stephen hesitated. He wasn't sure he had it in him. He held out a finger for Ray to hold, allowed himself to be sucked into the vortex of a baby's all-encompassing gaze.

Brenda was watching him, wanting him to take the baby. He resisted.

"You got to hold him," said Marcus. "He's your namesake, man. Stevie Ray."

Stephen eyed Marcus, mystified.

"Stevie Ray," he repeated. "Actually he's named after the guitar player Stevie Ray Vaughan."

"Don't tease," said Destiny. She turned to Stephen. "He really is named after you," she said. "The Ray came later."

Marcus's smile notched up a peg. "It's true, Stephen."

Stephen took the baby carefully, frightened at first by its fragile appearance and then surprised at how solid it really was. He remembered holding Toni when she was this young; the sweet smell, the fit inside your arms as if that were all that arms had ever been meant to do. The baby reached up to grab at his nose with almost translucent fingers.

"Hi," said Stephen. "Nice to meet you."

Marcus was beaming now, the bad news all behind him. Stephen could see it on his face; Marcus had what he wanted, the two families brought together, his own and his birth family. But what did Stephen have?

He held the baby close, but his thoughts were not sweetened by this intimacy. I am not your uncle, he thought. Your father is not my brother. He glanced coldly at Brenda. And she is not my mother. It was all he could think. It became like a pulse he kept to himself. Stephen Dark. There was nothing he could say. He just held on to the child as if it were holding him up, the only anchor keeping him from drifting away.

"Now do you get the picture?" asked Marcus. His glance darted from his child to Stephen and then back again. His eyes filled, suddenly, with something like grief.

"What do you mean?" asked Stephen.

"I mean, can you imagine, Stevie, somebody being so asinine that they'd leave a baby in the safekeeping of good karma?"

"They must have been totally zonked," said Destiny.

Suddenly, the whole tender little scene seemed to Stephen to have been manufactured to justify what Brenda had done. He handed Ray back to Destiny, who was nearest. He was shaking with rage.

"What if somebody took Stevie Ray?"

Brenda flinched.

"You can't steal babies and pretend nothing happened," he said. He didn't want to talk about this, let alone argue about it. The kitchen was too small, the Ark too small. He tried to shove his way past Marcus, but Marcus grabbed him by the arm.

"Let me go," he said.

"Listen to me, Steve."

"Who says I'm Steve? Is that my real name?"

Marcus looked perplexed. "Of course it is."

"How would you know?"

Marcus seemed tongue-tied. He turned to Brenda.

"It is your name, Stephen," she said.

"Stephen what?"

Brenda's eyes closed.

"My last name!" said Stephen. "I'm just asking you who I am!"

Brenda shook her head. "I don't know."

Stephen tried to shake his brother off, but Marcus held on tight.

"Let him go, Mar," said Destiny.

"No!" said Marcus. "I don't want to let him go."

Stephen tore Marcus's hand from his arm. He stepped

back out of his reach. "Why not?" he said, his voice raised, close to breaking. "You disappear for four years—not a word, not a peep—and suddenly *you* don't want *me* to go?"

Marcus turned away as if his face had been slapped. He looked hurt and angry and full of regret all at once. "You're right," he said. "I let you down, big time. Walked out on you." He turned to face Stephen. "I was pissed about Doug leaving. I was in and out of therapy. I was hot-headed, always have been. And there was something wrong in this house. I couldn't take it. Believe me, Stevie, I know how you feel."

Stephen shook his head very slowly. "No, you don't," he said. "Maybe, if you were really my brother, you'd know how I feel."

He couldn't look at Marcus or anyone, then; he could only leave. He was almost at the front door when Marcus caught up with him and grabbed him hard. His eyes were fierce but not cruel.

Stephen tried to shake himself free, but Marcus pinned him against the wall. Stephen could feel the tears coming, welling up. He had to get out of there. "I just need to be alone," he said.

"I'm not going to stop you," said Marcus. "But you get one thing straight, before you go. As far as I'm concerned, you *are* my brother. Nothing changes that. Nothing."

Then Marcus let him go and with one last penetrating glance, turned and walked back toward the kitchen.

Stephen didn't move for a moment. When he did, he stood with his hand gripping the front doorknob for a moment longer. In the kitchen Brenda was sobbing. Destiny and Marcus were trying to comfort her. Stephen let go of the handle. When he was perfectly sure that he could stand without fear of falling, he made his way to the hall table, found the phone book, flipped the pages until he located Hesketh Martin. His hand shaking, he wrote down her name and number. Then, pulling himself up tall, he walked back to the kitchen. They all looked at him as he handed the slip of paper to Marcus. It was all he could do. He left without a word.

Mordor

The Bogey trench coat lay on the forest floor where Stephen had discarded it the night of the letter of transit. It was soggy now. A drench coat. It looked as if maybe things were living in it. Stephen lifted a corner with his toe. A spider crawled out of one of the sleeves. He should take the coat home and hose it down. He doubted he would ever wear it again, but it deserved better than this. It had done the job that night. As flimsy a cover as it might have been, it had given him the courage to carry out a daring plan. Like the centurion armor had done for him at eleven, the disguise had been a warning to those who looked upon him.

"Look out! I am not who you think I am."

A disguise? What was he thinking? Stephen Fair was his disguise. This skin he was wearing was Stephen Fair's skin, not his own. All his conscious life, he had been living a false identity. If he could have, he would have torn it off right then—wriggled right out of it. For it felt like something foreign, something picked up off the forest floor sopping wet and crawling with bugs.

What sort of a poem can I make of myself without knowing my name? I am Stephen. Just Stephen. And what is there in that?

Step, hen, see, pen, steep.

Steep, the name Toni had given him. The name his best friend called him. That was something.

He looked up into the dazzle of spring sky. Above him, cradled in the arms of his oak tree, was the tree house. He placed his foot tentatively on the first rung. It was weathered and splintery. He reached up. He wondered if the ladder could possibly survive under the weight of him, burdened as he was.

He lifted himself onto the rung. It wobbled but held. Hardly a nail had been hammered in true; they were bent and flattened, clinging by so little to the living wood of the oak. And yet they held him.

No two rungs were the same. They were all off-cuts, scraps from the Ark. Stuff Doug hadn't needed anymore.

He slipped, grabbed a nearby branch; lost his footing, found it. Yet he wasn't scared. Maybe climbing was in his blood. Anyway, it wasn't like climbing in a dream. In a dream anything could happen.

Two more steps and he was there. Not so high as it had once seemed. He shinnied up onto the platform. If the ladder was in bad shape, the floor of the tree house was worse. It was covered with moldy leaves, moss, and bird droppings. He edged around on his butt to the safest-looking section, clearing a spot there.

In a corner there was an old suitcase with rusted locks and a torn cover. The locks would not budge, but when he pulled hard enough on the handle, the leather tore and he was able to peel back the top. Four years of water had seeped inside, frozen and thawed, heated up and dried, destroying the suitcase from the inside out. He had kept comic books there. They were now just so much pulp. Pulp fiction. Comic-book blood had stained the satin lining.

He edged over until he could lean against the tree trunk. It was evening now, the sun westering.

He closed his eyes, felt the air move beneath him, the leaves shiver above him, the sap rise in the tree at his back. He thought of being born into a tree house. These would have been the first feelings, the first sounds he would have known. After the sounds of his parents' voices, that is.

Two new words in his vocabulary: Yale and Sally. His parents. Well, his birth parents. And if the story was true, they hadn't been much else. If the story was true, he hadn't really been kidnapped so much as he had been saved. Like a bird, his mother had laid him in a nest and then flown off. It was Brenda who had incubated him, hatched him.

Brenda had never let him call her mother; now he knew why. And the idea of their family as an organic, flowing thing took on a whole new meaning. But she had stayed by him. If the story was true.

But why should he believe it was? Maybe they were only protecting him from an even crueler story. Maybe he had been lifted from a baby carriage in a park, bought on the black market, robbed from his cradle, his parents murdered in their bed!

Doubts foul and discouraging seized Stephen's imagination, but he cast them off. Wasn't this truth bad enough, without having to dream up a worse one?

Robbed. That's what he felt. Cheated. "I want my family," he said.

A sound from the woods seemed to answer him. He wasn't sure what it was, at first, why it had captured his attention. A birdsong in a forest full of birds. Then it dawned on him. It was a mourning dove. He sat up straight, listening, waiting as if it might actually speak to him. There it was again, so distinctively plaintive. He had heard that sound many times before, but not until that morning had he known what it was. Now its song was like a pale pinky-brown thread sewing this longest of all possible days together.

When he had walked up the driveway to the Ark he had looked up at the dead-tree flagpole. The flag Brenda had made so long ago was still flying, tattered and sunbleached though it might be. There were Noah and Mrs. Noah letting the dove go.

"Go find us some land," said Noah.

"You got it!" the dove replied.

Now here was the dove in Mordor. A kind of peace descended upon him.

The peace that had come with the mourning dove's song now firmed into resolve. He heaved himself over the edge and onto the ladder. Then he heard someone coming through the brush.

"Stephen? Are you here somewhere?"

It was Virginia. She was wearing her rubber boots and overalls.

He scuttled down the ladder. By the time he had dropped to the ground and dusted himself off, she was there and had discovered the trench coat.

"Your magic cape," she said. She crouched to look at it more closely. "It doesn't look so magic anymore."

She stood up, looked at him, shyly, he thought. He had never seen her look shy. She shoved her hands in her pockets.

"How did you find me?"

"Hung a right at Mirkwood," said Virginia. Then she looked around. The branches seemed hung with golden tinsel; the bush seemed on fire with setting sunlight. "It's beautiful down here," she said. "I thought Mordor was supposed to be a barren place. This is more like the elves' forest. What was it called?"

"Lothlorien," said Stephen, looking around. "Maybe you're right. I never thought of it that way."

Virginia cocked her head to one side, an unasked question. Stephen chose to leave it that way for the moment.

"How did you know I was here?"

"I got worried when I didn't hear from you. So I dropped by your place, all innocent like. You know, 'Can Stevie come out to play?'"

Stephen laughed, and it felt good.

"This tank with a ring through his eyebrow answered the door. He said you'd gone for a little walk. Is everything okay?"

"It's a long story," said Stephen, but he felt a quickening inside when he said it—he realized that he was dying to tell her. It was his story, after all. And if it hadn't happened, he wouldn't be here now. If it hadn't happened, there wouldn't have been any story. Not this story, anyway.

Virginia's eyes lit up. "Oh, and there was this woman who came to the door."

"A skinny redhead."

"No," said Virginia. "This beautiful older woman, in a long white cotton dress and Birkies. She had steel gray woolly hair. I think it was your witch lady."

Stephen was surprised at his relief to hear that Hesketh was at the house. "She's not really a witch," he said.

"Oh, but she'd make a perfect witch. She had this wise smile. If I was looking for a witch for a movie, I'd hire her for sure."

It was only then that Stephen noticed Virginia didn't have her camera. "Oh, that," she said. "It's not my blankie, you know."

Stephen raised an eyebrow.

"Well, that's what the counselor as much as said. Can you believe it!" She was bursting with her own story to tell, about her family's first therapy session the previous Thursday. She had, as promised, packed her videocam. First Marlo, at home, and then Lehmann, whom they met in the waiting room, tried to convince her that it was not appropriate, that the counseling session was a serious matter. She suggested they let the counselor decide. He, in turn, turned the question back to the Skyes.

So for almost half an hour they had argued about it, and the counselor had just watched and listened. He finally intervened when Lehmann started getting a bit "overanimated," but the counselor was smiling. "You folks sure know how to talk," he said, and he seemed very pleased.

"It was as if we'd passed the audition," said Virginia, "and now all we had to do was learn our parts."

"So, did you film the rest of the meeting?"

Virginia shook her head. "The guy asked me if I knew where the word camera came from. I didn't. So he told me that it came from the Latin word for room. That the first camera was called a camera obscura, meaning dark room. A darkroom where the film develops, right?" Stephen nodded. "Then," said Virginia moodily, "this guy says, 'When you're behind the lens of that camera, it's as though you're looking in at what's going on from someplace else.' Not really part of things. Some nerve, huh?"

Stephen nodded but couldn't think of anything to say to make her feel better.

"He made it sound as if I'm hiding behind the thing."

They walked on in silence, she brooding with resentment, he with anticipation. Then, just as they were nearing the point where their ways would part, some of the spirit returned to Virginia's face.

Stephen looked at her. Her eyes were beaming again, but her face looked different to him, somehow. She had revealed something to him and it had been hard. She had her own problems—her own family crisis, her own demons to wrestle with. He hadn't thought she needed much of anything, let alone something to hide behind. Maybe everybody did. So the hundred-watt smile right now meant a lot. He sucked it in, felt ready to face whatever was in store down the road. And then, realizing that Virginia might need the energy herself, he did his best to reflect some of the smile back at her.

She twirled around once in her oversized rubber boots. "What do you think?" she said. "Do I look different without it?"

"Totally," said Stephen. "But I'll get used to it."

As they walked out of Mordor, up the steep way to the meadow path, Stephen told her his story—the short form. They stood for an awkward, unspeaking moment at the top of the hill.

She looked at him with deep concern. "How are you

now?" she asked. It was something the locals said with the emphasis on the *now*, as if absolutely anything might have happened since they last saw you.

And Stephen answered the way the locals answered. "Fair to middlin'," he said.

The Rescue Remedy

4 drops star of Bethlehem
4 drops rock rose
4 drops impatiens
4 drops cherry plum
4 drops clematis

This is Brenda Fair.

That's what Hesketh Martin said. The star of Bethlehem was for shock, the rock rose was for great fear and for panic, the impatiens for tension, the cherry plum for hysteria, the clematis for just plain spaciness. This was Dr. Bach's rescue remedy. He had first used it on a fisherman who had only just survived a shipwreck. Brenda looked as if she had survived a shipwreck of her own. Only just.

She was on the poop deck when Stephen went to her. The poop deck was a screened-in porch off the master bedroom. You could see a long way from up there. To the south across the back garden and out into the woods, to the north a fair curve of the front driveway. Stephen paused on the threshold, staring out beyond Brenda, who did not turn to look at him when he arrived. In the dappled early-evening shadows, Marcus and Destiny were happily trudging hand in hand down the logging road, with Ray in his Snugli strapped to his father. They had left the Ark to Brenda and Stephen.

There were two rocking chairs on the poop deck. Brenda occupied one of them, a Mexican shawl around her shoulders. The vial of rescue remedy and a half-eaten orange on a plate lay at her feet. There was also a spent cup of something with a dead fly floating in it.

Stephen lowered himself carefully into the other rocker, making it stay perfectly still. Brenda looked at him, her face all puffy though she wasn't crying anymore. She held a tall glass of water in her lap, and Stephen wondered if it was filled with tears. She bent down, took the vial Hesketh had prepared for her, and squeezed several drops into the water.

"Hesketh told me it was time I took some of my own medicine," she said. Her voice and the joke were shaky but serviceable. "She thought that it was me who needed the medical attention. She was right. I've been so blind."

Stephen was going to speak; she stopped him. "Please." She held up her hand. "Let me say my piece, and then I promise I'll listen."

She paused. The wind in the treetops seemed to be blowing the setting sun around. Stephen caught the sound of laughter on the wind. It was Marcus, somewhere out there in the woods.

"There was something that didn't come up this afternoon. Something that happened before we left Santa Cruz. Doug insisted we go down to the cop shop—as he called it—to see if maybe Yale and Sally had been busted." She saw Stephen's eyes light up. "They weren't there, but I wanted you to know that we tried. I wanted you to know for two reasons. First of all, it was brave of Doug to go anywhere near a police station, considering his paranoia about getting arrested. He cared a lot about your welfare, Stephen. Secondly, since I don't want to hold anything back anymore, I wanted you to know how hard I tried to stop him."

Stephen looked surprised, confused. "Why?"

There were pinprick tears in Brenda's eyes. "Because I didn't want to find them."

Stephen leaned back stiffly in his chair. He wasn't sure which bothered him more, Brenda's guilty admission or Doug's trying to pawn him off.

"I guess Doug never really felt good about me being around."

Brenda shook her head. "That's not true. He was as good a father as he could be. He thought you were wonderful and he was always careful to treat you with the same respect he treated your . . . treated Mar and Toni."

Respect, thought Stephen. Not love.

"It was hard on him. I didn't think about that back at Tinkerpaw—the long-term effects. Doug went along with it for my sake. By the time we came to our senses and realized the magnitude of what we had done, we were stuck with you."

"Thanks."

Brenda closed her eyes and leaned her head back on the rocker. "Great choice of words, huh," she said, and the tenderness in her voice went a long way toward easing his resentment. "I think part of my guilt is that I've never been able to entirely convince myself that I abducted you only out of concern for your well-being. My worst fear is that I did it because I was so taken by you."

She paused, sat up, looked out the screen. Stephen followed her gaze. He saw nothing but caught an earful of music. Marcus singing. Brenda slumped back into her chair.

"You mustn't think you were the reason Doug left,

Stephen. He left because he had to move on. In the past, I'd always been ready to pack up and go along. But not anymore. This was my home.

"Anyway, it was a complex thing; all breakups are. But let's just say our guilty secret—our crime—always hung above the relationship like a thundercloud. And when we started to fall apart, the cloud burst.

"You overheard us arguing about Tinkerpaw. I never knew that until today. Maybe Marcus heard something, too. I guess there are some things too big to hide. He doesn't remember, but I can't help but think that over-hearing our powwows was what set him dreaming those terrible dreams. And then, there you were—his scribe!—writing it all down for him. I was horrified. I should have confessed right away, but I couldn't bring my-self to. My whole world was crumbling around me. I was so afraid Doug would take you—all three of you—and leave me with nothing.

"I panicked. I revealed enough about Tinkerpaw that the psychiatrist might be able to help Marcus. But what he needed, of course, was the whole truth."

She took another long drink from her glass of water. It was almost empty. Her voice, when she spoke again, was almost empty, too.

"I don't regret what I did, Stephen." With an effort, Brenda kept her voice under control. "I only hope you don't hate me," she said.

Stephen watched the flies, dormant all winter, buzzing and bumbling against the inside of the screen. Stupid. Co-matose. Lying on their backs on the sill and floor, kicking the air. A thousand questions came to mind, but they would have to wait. There was only one thing he had to say right now.

But how? The stage was his and he knew his lines, but how parched he felt. He saw Brenda's half-eaten orange. He picked it up and pulled off a thick wedge. The skin was parchmentlike, hardening off. He bit into it, and through the rent in the dry skin, sweet juice flowed into his mouth. He swallowed hard. He could speak now.

"I don't hate you," he said. "Hate is like a big heavy steel door."

He cleared his throat. He needed to say what had come to him on the road that afternoon, been distilled in the tree house. The one sure conclusion he had reached.

"I want my family back," he said.

Brenda sighed raggedly, like a woman on trial listening to an inescapable verdict. "I understand," she said.

"I want my mother and father," said Stephen.

Below them Marcus, Ray, and Destiny came back into view. They had taken a circular route and entered the garden near the pond. They walked toward the dinghy. Stephen could just hear Marcus's voice as he pointed things out. "This shed is where we lived when we first moved here."

"I'll help you any way I can," said Brenda at last. Her voice was calm. "I read a story in a magazine about a kid finding his birth parents on the Net."

Marcus had opened the dinghy; Destiny stepped inside.

"No, you don't understand," said Stephen.

"You have to start somewhere," said Brenda. "It won't be easy."

"I don't mean Yale and Sally," said Stephen.

For a moment he thought that someone had turned up the volume of the flies, for their buzzing suddenly was deafening.

"*This* family," he said. "I want this family back."

Now what he was saying dawned on her. But almost immediately the light in her eyes was extinguished. "Oh, Stephen. You can't expect that Doug and I could ever get back together. He's got a new family—"

Stephen's fists came down with a bang on the arms of his chair. "I'm not a kid," he said. "I know he's not coming back. But maybe I'll go see him sometime, like Marcus did. If I feel like it. Who knows."

Brenda nodded thoughtfully. "That would be good," she said.

Stephen shrugged. Doug was the least of his concerns right now. He took a deep breath. "And I want Marcus back."

Again Brenda nodded. Her cheeks flushed at the implication that she had been keeping Marcus from him. "Of course," she said.

Which brought Stephen to the last of his demands, the most difficult. "I'd like to try out a little experiment," he said, hesitantly. "I don't know if it will work."

"Anything," said Brenda. She was leaning forward, her elbows on her knees, not looking at him, sensing his uncertainty, giving him some room.

He cleared his throat. "I'd like Brenda to take a holiday," he said. "She needs a break."

"You want me to leave," she said.

"Not exactly. It's just that I've kind of had enough of Brenda for the time being. You know what I mean?"

Brenda bowed her head. "I know what you mean."

Stephen took a deep breath. This was hard. "I wouldn't mind having a mom around, though." He watched her face—what he could see of it—saw it change. "It's a role-playing thing," he said, quickly now, wanting to get it over with. "You have to answer to Mom." She was smiling. "If you're interested in the job," he added.

Her eyes were squeezed shut. She was nodding her head, then she hid her face in her hands so that he couldn't tell anymore if she was laughing or crying.

"What do you think?"

She couldn't speak at first. She just kept nodding. Then her voice came out as a kind of gulp. "Mom it is," she said.

"Good," said Stephen. And he let his rocking chair go, started rocking because he had nothing pressing left to say—nothing that couldn't wait—and rocking seemed a good thing to do.

A car pulled into the driveway. It was Dee's father delivering Toni.

"I called them," said Brenda. "Just after you left. I wasn't sure what was going to happen—whether you'd even come back—but I knew I wanted her home where she belongs."

Amen, thought Stephen.

Toni was saying good-bye to Dee through the car window. She had her yellow ducky backpack on. Dee's father pointed up to the poop deck and waved. Toni waved, too.

Stephen and Brenda waved back.

Dee's father drove out of the driveway just as Marcus and Destiny walked around from the back garden.

Toni walked directly up to them and started asking them questions about the baby. She couldn't possibly have recognized her brother, for she had only been a baby herself when he left home. And from where Stephen sat, it didn't seem as if Marcus was in any hurry to introduce himself, even if he'd had a chance. It was clear Toni had only one thing on her mind, and soon enough, Marcus was digging

Stevie Ray out of his Snugli and handing him to his little aunt.

Baby Ray dangled from her arms, his shoulders squished up against his fat cheeks. The parents hovered, but Toni had a good strong grip on the child. She looked toward the poop deck, where her mother and Stephen were little more than familiar sihouettes in the setting sun.

"You should see this," she called to them. "Somebody brought us a baby."

Epilogue

Summer was chasing spring right out of town. Stephen had slept through a lot of it. Slept like a log. Slept as if he had a lot to catch up on.

He woke up long enough to take his exams. Another school year was in the books. And Marcus, just home from a long road trip, was coming to the Ark with Des and Stevie Ray for the weekend. There was even some talk that they might bring Nan with them. Stephen was heading through the woods to the Skyes' house to bring Virginia home for dinner, although the thought of Nan, Brenda, Destiny, Virginia, and Toni all in the same house together—let alone the same room—was pretty daunting. But it was the Ark, after all; it was meant to hold large numbers.

There was going to be another big theme party at the Skyes' in a week or two. They were going to watch *The African Queen,* and Marlo was going to make food from Central Africa. Dom was threatening to come as a headhunter.

Lehmann was home again. He had sold the hog and gotten himself an old sports car, an MGB with real leather seats. The real leather was torn here and there and the body needed work. "So does mine," Lehmann had said. But the big thing about that little car was that there was room for Marlo in it, and Virginia, too, if she didn't mind curling up in a backseat about the size of a shoe box.

The woods were lush with summer greenery and riotous with birdsong. Stephen listened for a mourning dove, but he could barely hear himself think.

He passed by the path that led into Mordor. The way was already overgrown with bramble. Impenetrable. It would take a lot of work to get back in there, work in which Stephen had no interest these days. He had outgrown the tree house.

He headed on, whistling a bit until he reached his and Dom's place in the woods. And there, to his shock, he saw a stranger. An adult. He moved closer, sneaking up on the intruder. Then he smiled.

It was Lehmann. It had been hard to tell at first, for his hair was chopped short.

He appeared to be attaching a new string to the cup that hung from the branch above the pool. The pool was back to its normal size; the waters had receded. He saw Stephen and was equally startled.

"Do you know this place?" he asked.

"Oh, sure," said Stephen. Then he remembered a line from *Casablanca*, a line that Lehmann had used on him, and he tried to say it just like Bogart. "I came here for the waters."

Lehmann laughed, his gold filling catching the light.

He let the cup dangle from its branch. It spun around until all the kinks were out of the new string.

"That's a really bad haircut," said Stephen.

"Thanks," said Lehmann, rubbing his hand through his shorn locks. "I did it myself. I decided I'd check out being an adult for a while. If that turns out okay, I'll apply for tribal elder."

Stephen went over to Lehmann and nodded at the string. "We always wondered who did that."

Lehmann looked up at him. He had to shield his eyes from the sun, but in the shadow of his hand there appeared a satisfied look on his face. "Glad to be of some small service," he said.

A bigger service than you know, thought Stephen. Sometime he would tell him that. Thank him for being there, thank him for staying. Maybe, some rainy day when there was nothing better to do, he would find in Lehmann's name the right words to thank him.

Lehmann stood up, stretched his back.

"I grew up nearby," he said. "Before Meadowview Acres came along. On a farm, believe it or not. It's gone now. I spent a lot of time here."

The two of them surveyed the woods for a moment.

"So you're the one who left the cup," said Stephen.

Lehmann shook his head. "Heck no." He bent down again, took a long, slow drink, then refreshed the cup and handed it to Stephen. Stephen drank deeply. Nothing was so cold. Nothing so fine or clear.

"Then who?" asked Stephen.

Lehmann shrugged. "It's probably been here forever."